"You're definitely pregnant?"

"There's no doubt. Eight weeks along."

There was silence. Was he counting back the days to their time in the hotel in Bloomsbury? "How do you feel about the pregnancy?"

"Shock. Disbelief. Acceptance. And finally, joy. Yes, joy. It might surprise you, considering what I've said to you before, but I...I want this baby very much. I'm not nineteen this time. The prospect of a baby from the perspective of twenty-nine with my own business is very different from me as a nineteen-year-old student."

"That's quite a turnaround," he said.

"Back then...as we said, it was a different world. I'm different. At a different stage of life."

"What role do you expect me to play?"

No instant proposal of marriage this time. "Whatever we sort out. Between us. You can have as much access as you want." She had adored her father and would do all she could to make sure Stefanos played a role in her child's life.

Another pause. "I need to think about this," he said. "It's quite a shock."

Her voice caught. "It was for me too."

Dear Reader,

Have you ever met a person you like instantly but have to wait for your chance to get to know them? Claudia Eaton, the heroine of *Pregnancy Shock for the Greek Billionaire*, was one such person for me.

Claudia is the best friend and business partner of Kitty Clements, heroine of my last book, *Second Chance with His Cinderella*. Beautiful, talented Claudia doesn't have a lot of luck with men. Could that be because she never quite got over her first love, gorgeous billionaire Stefanos Adrastos, whom she met as a teenager on a vacation in Greece? Ten years later, a chance meeting brings them together, and old passions ignite but old hurts also surface. When Stefanos whisks Claudia away to a beautiful Greek island, can they work their way through past pain so first love becomes forever love?

Kitty pops in and out of Claudia's story and so do Dell and Alex, from an earlier book, *Conveniently Wed to the Greek*. This story is all about Claudia and Stefanos, but I liked giving their friends a little input too!

I hope you enjoy Claudia and Stefanos's reunion story!

Warm regards,

Kandy

Pregnancy Shock for the Greek Billionaire

—

Kandy Shepherd

Recycling programs
for this product may
not exist in your area.

ISBN-13: 978-1-335-73678-9

Pregnancy Shock for the Greek Billionaire

Copyright © 2022 by Kandy Shepherd

Harlequin Enterprises ULC
22 Adelaide St. West, 41st Floor
Toronto, Ontario M5H 4E3, Canada
www.Harlequin.com

Printed in U.S.A.

Kandy Shepherd swapped a career as a magazine editor for a life writing romance. She lives on a small farm in the Blue Mountains near Sydney, Australia, with her husband, daughter and lots of pets. She believes in love at first sight and real-life romance—they worked for her! Kandy loves to hear from her readers. Visit her at kandyshepherd.com.

Books by Kandy Shepherd

Harlequin Romance

Christmas at the Harrington Park Hotel

Their Royal Baby Gift

Sydney Brides

Gift-Wrapped in Her Wedding Dress
Crown Prince's Chosen Bride
The Bridesmaid's Baby Bump

Conveniently Wed to the Greek
Stranded with Her Greek Tycoon
Best Man and the Runaway Bride
Second Chance with the Single Dad
Falling for the Secret Princess
One Night with Her Millionaire Boss
From Bridal Designer to Bride
Second Chance with His Cinderella

Visit the Author Profile page
at Harlequin.com for more titles.

To three lovely friends I've met through the world of romance writing: Cathleen Ross for her constant support; Efthalia Pegios for her help with Greek language across several books; and to wonderful reader Helen Sibbritt—Helen, this gorgeous Greek hero is for you!

Praise for
Kandy Shepherd

CHAPTER ONE

CLAUDIA EATON STARED at the name on the client booking form for so long the type began to blur. *Stefanos Adrastos*. It couldn't be him. Impossible. It must be a common enough Greek name. A coincidence. That sudden jolt of her heart at the sight of his name meant nothing. She forced a deep calming breath.

The booking for her company, People Who Pack, had come just days ago from a relocation agency that regularly contracted her to pack up their clients' residences. A last-minute cancellation had allowed her to slot it in for this morning. She'd hastily noted the address, but hadn't had time to take notice of the name buried further down in the details provided by the agency. It was one of many of the smaller jobs that were the bread and butter of her business.

If she had noticed the name there was no way she would be standing on the steps of the imposing converted Georgian house, waiting to be buzzed up to an apartment. She would have sent someone else from PWP to check on his identity. She could now, having got this far, turn around and flee—pretend she'd got the time wrong. But PWP had a reputation to uphold. The relocation service sent a lot of business her way, and she couldn't afford to let them down. Not just because the name of the client struck a chord from her past.

This Stefanos Adrastos—surely not *her* Stefanos Adrastos, who was a long time and an ocean of heartbreak ago—was moving his personal effects from an apartment in Bloomsbury to an address in Athens. Her Stefanos had never wanted to live anywhere but Greece—certainly not central London. He was the heir to his family's shipping business, probably holding the reins of it by now.

She tried to convince herself that this client named Stefanos Adrastos was an elderly scholar—this area was within a hop, skip and a jump of the British Museum, the British Library, numerous university colleges and the homes of many lauded literary figures. Or perhaps a young student whose wealthy parents could afford accommodation a cut above the usual student digs.

The sooner she discovered for sure that this man was not her first love—last seen ten years ago when she was nineteen—the better. Then she could get on with the job she'd been contracted to do.

Nevertheless, her voice was an unrecognisable croak as she spoke through the intercom to introduce herself as 'Claudia from PWP'. The imposing front door swung open to a marble-tiled foyer. She took the small elevator to apartment number three, which took up the entire top floor. Before her knuckles could rap on the door, it swung open. A tall, broad-shouldered, dark-haired man stood there.

She recognised him instantly.

Him. Stefanos. It was him.

Claudia stared at him, unable to believe it really was *her* Stefanos and that he was here in London. *After all this time.* The man who had been her first love, whom she'd thought she could never live without—until she'd had to.

His smile of welcome froze as he stared right back at her. 'You,' he said gruffly.

'Y-yes, me,' she stuttered, unable to say anything more substantial.

'Claudia. Just Claudia. No surname. That's who I was told was coming to pack for me.'

His English was perfect, as it had been back then, with just a trace of a charming accent. As he had done then, he called her *Cloudia*, in the European way, rather than Claudia—she had used to like it.

'I didn't know it was you. Or I... I...' She was going to say *Or I wouldn't have come*—but could she have resisted the opportunity to see him again? Even after the bitterness of their parting. Would *he* have cancelled if he'd known it was *her*?

She couldn't tear her gaze away from him. Ten years had wrought differences. The last time she'd seen Stefanos he'd been a boy of twenty. Now he was very much a man—black curls cut short, the dark stubble on his chin halfway to a beard, his skin a pale olive rather than a deep tan. He seemed taller, more substantial. *Even more handsome.*

Shock piled upon shock: the shock of his presence, of the undisguised hostility in his eyes, of her own visceral response to him. *She'd never forgotten him.* A flush burned hot on her face and neck—a curse that came with red hair and fair skin. She'd never fainted in her life, but she suddenly felt woozy and clutched onto the doorframe for support. In doing so, she lost her grip on the clipboard containing the paperwork for this packing job. It hit the ground and papers scattered across the threshold and into his apartment.

'S-sorry,' she stuttered, still barely able to claim her own voice.

She bent down to collect the papers from the

floor at the same time he did, and their shoulders collided. The action brought them close… intimately close…her cheek nearly touching his face, his scent achingly familiar. He was *too* close for the strangers they now were to each other.

Abruptly, she stepped back to break the contact. 'Sorry,' she said again, although ten years ago he hadn't wanted to hear her apologies.

'Let me get them,' he said shortly.

She was too dazed to protest, rather just watched him gather the pages that had come loose from the clipboard. His hands were as she remembered, strong and well-shaped, and she forced back the memories of how skilfully they had played her body. There was no wedding band, although that didn't necessarily mean anything—she'd learned that painful lesson.

He handed over the clipboard and the papers and she took them, not attempting to sort them into any kind of order, just opening the clip and shoving them haphazardly under it.

'Th-thank you,' she stuttered.

His gaze was intent. 'You're packing boxes these days? What happened to the career in international hotels you planned?'

He remembered her dream. Not surprisingly, perhaps, when it had stood in the way of the life he'd dreamed of. Their dreams had collided.

She looked up at him. 'I had it. I did it. Now I'm doing this. People Who Pack is my own business.'

She was in partnership with her friend Kitty Clements, although Kitty had been more an investor than an active partner since she'd fallen in love with their client Sir Sebastian Delfont and married him three months ago in February.

'We're very successful and I like being my own boss,' Claudia said, struggling to suppress the note of defensiveness in her voice.

When he spoke, his voice sounded forced… indifferent. 'Still, I'm surprised. That career meant everything to you.'

More than he had meant to her.

Or that was what he'd said, his voice reverberating with pain and anger, when they'd broken up. She'd been nineteen, he twenty when they'd met on vacation in Santorini. A holiday romance that had quickly deepened into something more intense. But everything she'd wanted for her future hadn't been centred around Athens. She'd wanted him, all right—she'd thought she could never have had enough of him. But at the age of nineteen she had seen the possibilities for her life stretching far on the horizon, while Stefanos's vision had been constricted and defined by his family.

He'd been content to stay in Greece, she had ached to see the world.

Hers had been a dream that ran deep. Her parents had managed a popular, traditional-style pub in a picture-perfect Devon village. It also provided accommodation, and travellers from far and wide had passed through. Even as a small child Claudia had loved being part of it all. She'd asked favourite visitors to send her a postcard from where they lived—be it in Britain, Europe or further afield. A surprising number of people had done so. The wall covered in postcards from around the world had become a feature of the pub. And it had ignited in her a thirst to see as many of those places as she could.

Her father had used to joke that she had hospitality in her veins. It was true. All she'd ever wanted to do was work in hotel management and travel the world.

But in later years her dream career had soured. She'd found limits on her ambition. It hadn't just been the realisation that she would get nowhere in family-run hotels, or that the big international hotels were too anonymous for her taste. Her last role had become more nightmare than dream because of a relationship with a colleague that hadn't ended well.

PWP had signalled a new beginning for her

and Kitty, who'd had her name blackened by a vengeful boss.

'What about you?' she said to Stefanos, forcing her voice to show a polite interest with no hint of the raging curiosity she felt. 'I'm surprised to see you living in Bloomsbury rather than Athens.'

They hadn't kept in touch after she'd gone back to England at the end of summer.

'I never want to hear from you again,' he'd said grimly.

She hadn't believed he'd meant it. Not after all they'd shared. But Stefanos had been deadly serious. His social media had been blocked to her, his phone number disconnected, her emails to him had bounced. It had hurt, but eventually she'd come to terms with it. She'd stopped doing internet searches on him a long time ago.

'I've been studying archaeology,' he said.

Her brows lifted in surprise. 'I thought you'd be running the shipping business by now.' Hadn't he said that was his destiny?

'Things changed,' he said gruffly.

So many things had changed since he'd last seen Claudia, Stefanos thought, still shocked almost senseless by the sudden appearance on his doorstep of a red-haired vision from his past.

Claudia herself had changed so much it had

taken a moment for him to recognise this woman as the vivacious English teenager who had captivated him from the moment she'd first served him his favourite Greek beer in a bar in Santorini. What hadn't changed was how beautiful he found her.

He was unable to tear his eyes away from her, once so familiar on his boat in a skimpy bikini, in his bed wearing nothing at all. Her waist-length red hair had darkened to a rich auburn, cut to her shoulders in a sleek bob, and the freckles scattered across her nose had faded to an English winter pale. But it was in her eyes where he saw the most change. They were still as blue as the Aegean Sea, but where once they had sparkled with laughter and mischief they now seemed guarded and wary.

Was it because of her surprise at seeing him? Or because she had seen more of life's darker side since they'd parted. Who knew? And why should he care?

'What changed?' she asked.

Should he tell her? Did she have a right to know what had happened since those dark days when she had left him nursing his wounded pride and his broken heart? Mentally he shrugged. He'd put Claudia Eaton behind him long ago. It was of no consequence what she knew about his life.

'My father died when I was twenty-four. My mother and I sold the company.'

'Oh. I'm so sorry.' Her voice, which had seemed stilted and ill at ease, now warmed with genuine sympathy. 'I remember how much you admired him. You must have been devastated.'

Why did she have to be so nice? To immediately think of how the death of his father had affected him personally rather than allude to how much he had inherited—as other women had done? But then Claudia had always been thoughtful and kind, unimpressed by his fortune. It had made the pain of losing her run even deeper. He remembered her own father had died when she was fifteen.

'Devastated about losing my father? Yes.' His powerful, energetic father had been felled by a sudden massive heart attack. Stefanos swallowed hard to contain the burst of grief he still felt at the thought of his loss. 'The company? Not so much.'

She frowned. 'You were the only child…your father's successor.'

She remembered that? Not surprising, perhaps, when the family responsibilities he hadn't been able to evade—hadn't wanted to evade, out of his powerful sense of duty—had skewered any hope of a future with wanderlust-fired Claudia.

Stefanos had grown up knowing his future was running the Adrastos Shipping Group—just as his father himself had taken over from his own father, Stefanos's grandfather. Stefanos had an inbred aptitude for business, but he hadn't expected to step into his father's shoes so soon. His mother—daughter of a shipping magnate herself—had sensed his ambivalence about his role. When they'd had an offer for the company they'd agreed to take it, divesting themselves of their tankers and container ships while keeping the lucrative yacht charter business that reflected his own interests.

'It was what I wanted,' he said.

Silence hung between them for a beat too long.

Claudia cleared her throat. She hugged her clipboard with its out-of-order papers to her chest. 'I'm glad it all worked out for you. Now, I need to get started on your packing job...' She paused and looked up to him, her blue eyes wary. 'Unless it's awkward having me here? If you'd prefer, I could send another packer from the company.'

'Don't do that,' he said—too suddenly.

'Seriously,' she said. 'I have an excellent packer who lives not far from here. She can be here within the hour.'

He shook his head. 'I haven't got an hour to

waste. There's a lot to pack before the removal company comes tomorrow.'

No way would he admit, now that Claudia had come back into his life so unexpectedly, that he was reluctant to let her out of it too quickly. He had nursed his bitterness against her for a long time before finally letting it go. But seeing her here, now, brought back old emotions, raw and painful. She'd had such grand plans for her life—so much grander, it had seemed, than a billionaire's son could offer her—and yet here she was, packing boxes like one of the domestic staff at his Athens mansion.

Why?

His mind was churning with unspoken questions. Was she married? She didn't wear a ring… Did she have children? Did she ever regret walking away from everything he'd offered her?

'I'll get started on the packing, then' she said. 'Just point me in the right direction.'

Her tone was brisk and impersonal. If she was as disconcerted as he was by this unexpected meeting, she certainly didn't show it. He would do the same.

CHAPTER TWO

IT WAS ONLY with an enormous effort of will that Claudia was able to mask how shaken she was by this out-of-the-blue encounter with Stefanos. All the casual repartee she usually engaged in with a client deserted her. Because while he was indeed a client—and deserving of her full attention—he was also her first love and he had hurt her badly. That made it terribly awkward. And the way he was glowering at her didn't make it any easier.

She was still desperately trying to get her head around the reality of it. Stefanos. Here in London. The man who had ghosted her so thoroughly but whom she had never forgotten. On occasion she'd fantasised about seeing him again—of course she had. But in her fantasies she had been looking her best, composed and confident, with hair, make-up, everything perfect. Not feeling at a distinct disadvantage in trainers, leggings, and a baggy T-shirt with the hot pink PWP logo emblazoned on it. Her work clothes were comfortable and practical, but hardly the outfit she would have chosen to wear for her first meeting with him in ten years.

She was still outside the door and he stood just inside, looming over her like a gatekeeper, formidable in black jeans and dark olive green linen shirt. She'd forgotten how very black his hair was—his beard too. His eyes were half narrowed, as if he were judging her. Judging her on how she looked…how she had changed. Judging her, too, for her job. He would surely see it as a step down in the world, while she saw having her own business as an act of empowerment.

She didn't want to be judged. Not by him—not by anyone.

Head held high, she stepped forward to cross the threshold of his apartment.

Meticulously polite, Stefanos stood back to allow her through. She was intensely aware of his presence, his scent, the sheer masculinity of him. Her arm brushed against his as she passed by. She had to fight not to jerk it back. Not because she found his touch distasteful, but because of the powerful jolt of awareness ignited by that merest contact.

She caught her breath. *Did he feel it?*

Their relationship had been intensely physical. From the moment she'd met him, she'd wanted him. There'd been something about his good looks, his confidence, the touch of arrogance that had seen him assume—correctly—that she'd felt the same way he did. They'd spent every moment they could making love, their appetite for each other never sated.

Did he remember?

Each evening she had pushed through her summer vacation job in that bar, impatient for the end of her shift so she could throw herself into his arms and spend the rest of her time with him.

He had always been there, waiting for her on the cobblestoned street outside the whitewashed restaurant with its blue-painted furniture, which had overlooked the caldera—the submerged volcanic crater. She'd never questioned why he didn't work…why he had the most amazing yacht for his personal use. She had been well and truly head over heels in love with him before she'd discovered he was the son of one of the wealthiest men in Greece and heir to an immense shipping fortune. It had made no difference. He'd been just her beautiful, wonderful, perfect Stefanos. Until everything had changed.

Now here he was in the middle of London, where she could have passed him on the street, on a bus, and never known he was nearby. And she had never felt more uncomfortable. He seemed none too happy about her surprise presence in his apartment, yet he had refused her offer to get another packer. Should she read anything into that?

Stefanos directed her down a short corridor. It opened into a spectacular living room that had been stripped bare of all extraneous detail and was simply an architectural white space. Furnishings were starkly simple—all white and pale timber—highlighted by Greek archaeological artefacts mounted on marble blocks, an imposing pottery urn that must surely be worthy of pride of place in a museum, and a series of framed antique maps of the ancient world on the walls.

It was so striking she had to stifle a gasp of admiration. But she didn't say anything. First, because it was PWP policy not to comment on a client's possessions. Second, because she didn't know how Stefanos would take it. Did he own the apartment? Had it been designed to his taste? Would he value her opinion? It was safer to stick to her policy of being politely impersonal and show no indication of her inner turmoil.

She glanced at the neatly stacked folded boxes and packing material placed along one wall and felt reassured by their familiarity. They were what she and Kitty jokingly called the tools of their trade. She could do this. She could be a complete professional. She would not take a step out of place.

'Your people delivered the packing materials yesterday afternoon,' Stefanos said. 'There are more in the other rooms.'

'I'd like to see them,' she said, studiously avoiding catching his eye.

With only the minimum of words, he showed her around the spacious luxury apartment. She couldn't help but admire his back view, which hadn't changed from the days when he'd been clad in a pair of board shorts and nothing else and she'd teased him that he had the best male butt in Greece. Or those times when he'd worn no clothes at all, and he'd only had to look at her for her to melt with desire for him.

She forced her gaze away from his too-well-remembered body and back to the apartment. All the rooms were designed with the same white minimalism. She made appropriate comments about the contents that required packing, while hiding her intense curiosity. Back then he'd been so keen on family, yet she could detect no sign of a female presence here, or of children.

But again she didn't dare comment. There was something forbidding about Stefanos that had not been there when he was twenty. It curbed any thought she might have had of engaging with him. They'd never been short of words and laughter back then—not just with each other, but with the circle of other young people from around the world, lured by the beauty and mystique of the Greek islands. Now it was a struggle to choke out the bare minimum of words required to get her job done.

She followed him back to the living room. 'I understand the furniture and electrical appliances are to remain, but the books and ornaments and personal possessions of the resident are to be packed,' she said, in her best PWP voice. 'Household linens and kitchen equipment also to remain.'

'Correct.'

Could he be more terse if he tried?

'Will you be on hand to answer any questions I might have?'

'I will be in my study. You can pack up that room last.'

She nodded. 'I'll start here in the living room.'

'I'll leave you to it,' he said, turning on his heel.

Claudia was both relieved and disappointed after he left the room. She couldn't have borne it if he'd watched her as she worked, yet the room seemed empty without his commanding presence. She hadn't bitten her fingernails for years, but she had to fight the urge to nibble on her thumbnail at the very least.

How could she deal with this? She decided to pretend she wasn't working for her first love but rather the crusty old scholar she had at first imagined her client Stefanos Adrastos to be. Not tall and handsome and dynamic, but stooped, with a long silver beard and rheumy eyes behind metal-rimmed glasses.

She couldn't help but smile to herself at the thought.

But her smile quickly drooped at the corners and she felt the sting of tears. It was no good. Her thoughts were filled with *her* Stefanos. She had loved him so much. *Adored him.* It had ended with them both hurting each other. But that had been ten years ago. Wasn't it natural for her to want to know what had happened to him in the meantime? To ask how he had ended up studying archaeology in London, seemingly with no wife or family? Perhaps he had a wife and children back in Athens. If he did, she would like to know—it was what he had wanted back then.

Surely they could have a civil conversation that acknowledged that they had a past, even if they hadn't managed a future?

Claudia started to pack a shelf of glossy art and history books. Beautiful, expensive books. She picked up a handsome tome on the treasures of Sutton Hoo, the famous archaeological site in Suffolk. Was Stefanos here to study only British archaeology? There was an important archaeological site in Santorini, but she didn't remember him showing any interest in it at the time they'd met. He'd been too focused on his future in Adrastos Shipping—and, she reminded herself, on her.

She worked quickly and skilfully, concentrating on her work and refusing to think about Stefanos—although surrounded by his possessions that was extremely difficult.

She was taping up the third box when he strode into the room, startling her, making her turn. She couldn't help but stare at him afresh. Was her tongue hanging out? *He was hot.* Even hotter than he'd been when she'd fallen so hard for him. For a moment she wished she didn't have that history with him, that he was a handsome stranger who she could flirt with a little and find out more about.

PWP had had a no-dating-the-clients rule. Kitty had broken that rule in a spectacular manner— now she was Lady Kitty Delfont. Which kind of gave Claudia a pass to do the same if she wanted. So far no client had stirred the slightest interest in her...

'I can't sit in there while you do this work,' Stefanos said tersely, gesturing with his hand at the boxes. 'It's not right.'

Slowly, she put down her packing tape gun, took a step away from the box. 'It's my job, and I'm an expert at packing valuables.'

'It's hard physical work.'

'Which I am totally up for.'

She flexed an arm to show off the muscles she was so proud of. The job kept her fit—although that didn't stop her from going to the gym as well, to keep her strong. A strained back could spell disaster in her business.

'Let me at least help you,' he said, sounding very much as if packing boxes was the last thing he wanted to do.

She shook her head. 'Not a good idea. There's a good chance you'll invalidate your insurance if you do. You have employed me to do this.'

He scowled. 'No. I employed a removal company. They recommended packers. I did not employ you. I would not have—'

'You would not have employed the Claudia assigned to your job if you'd known it was me?'

He looked about to answer but she spoke over him. It would be too painful to hear him say yes.

'That's where we're different—as we always *were* very different. I didn't know you were the client. But even once I suspected it might be the Stefanos Adrastos I used to know, I didn't turn tail and slink away. I thought about it—trust me, I thought about it... But I stayed. And I stayed because I was curious to see what kind of man you'd grown up to be...how you'd lived your life and if...and if you were happy.'

* * *

Stefanos met her gaze, it seemed she was still as direct as she'd been back then. Not afraid to be outspoken and state her opinions, even if they differed from his. He'd liked that about her. So different from the girls who'd thought the way to dating a billionaire's son was to echo his opinions, to acquiesce with whatever he wanted.

'Of *course* I'm happy,' he said immediately. He scoffed at the thought that he could be anything other than happy. 'Why wouldn't I be?'

Her eyes widened. 'How could I have known the answer to that?'

Because ten years ago she had made him happy.

The thought struck him like a punch to the gut. He had never been as happy as those weeks with her in Santorini—not before, not since. It had been a vacation fling, he reminded himself, of no real significance. That was all it had been to her, anyway.

He folded his arms tightly in front of his chest, rocked back on his heels. 'Let me assure you my life is in a very good place. I don't want for anything and I'm doing exactly the work I want to do since we sold Adrastos Shipping.'

He had inherited so much money he never needed to work again, although he didn't have it in him to be idle. He'd appointed an excellent manager to the yacht charter business so he'd been able to take a year off to pursue his interest in archaeology with an aim of eventually earning a PhD. And yet…she'd hit a raw nerve.

'What about you?' he said.

'Me? Happy? Of course I am. I love having my own business, being my own boss.' She paused. Then gave a short brittle laugh that surprised him. 'We've both talked about work. Is that all we need to make us happy?'

'Satisfaction with work is important. But of course there is more. Family. Friends.' Family was so very important—which was why her attitude ten years ago had stunned him.

'Of course,' she echoed. 'Are you married?'

He should have expected that question but still it sideswiped him.

'Not now.'

She frowned. 'What do you mean "not now"?'

'Just that. I was married. Now I'm divorced. Single.'

'I'm sorry,' she said.

'I'm not sorry,' he said. 'It's a great relief.'

'Still, it's sad when a marriage ends…they generally start with expectations of happiness.'

'My last marriage was all about lies and deception.' He spoke through gritted teeth.

She put her hand up in a halt sign. 'Hold that. You just said your *last* marriage?'

Inwardly he cursed his misstep.

'There have been more than one?'

'I have been divorced twice.'

Divorced twice by the age of thirty. Not something he liked to boast about.

'Oh…' Claudia said.

'Why do you say "oh"?'

She shrugged. 'I don't know, really. Just to buy time. I'm gobsmacked that you've been married and divorced twice. And you've only just turned thirty.'

She'd remembered that his birthday was in March. Hers was in November—a date it seemed he'd been unable to forget.

'Both marriages were mistakes,' he said. *Massive mistakes.* The second an even worse mistake than the first. 'There are good reasons why they ended in divorce.'

Claudia looked at him expectantly. There was an unspoken question in her eyes, dancing around the corners of her pretty mouth: *Tell me those good reasons. C'mon. Spill.* He remembered she'd used to do that. She was a master of the silent question. Even after ten years, he remembered. Back then he had answered all her questions—had known she wouldn't give up teasing and wheedling and probing until he had. He had no intention of doing so today.

'Not reasons I care to disclose.'

'Right. Of course not,' she said. She paused before she launched into her next question. 'Any children?'

Of course she would ask that.

'No.' He kept his voice studiously neutral.

'That's a blessing, then.'

He stared at her. 'Surely you must realise I don't see it that way.'

He had wanted children, but neither marriage had brought them. Now it seemed likely he would never have a child. His two ugly marriages had made him vow never to marry again.

She flushed high on her cheekbones. 'I meant it must have been easier to divorce if there wasn't custody to battle over.'

'I take it you're not divorced?'

'Yes. I mean, no. I'm not divorced.'

'Because you haven't married?'

'Right first time.' She slipped off the protective work glove from her left hand and waggled her bare fingers. 'See?'

'So you haven't softened your stance on marriage since we last met?' He wasn't the only man who hadn't managed to put a ring on her finger. For some perverse reason that pleased him.

'No. Perhaps a little bit… For other people. Not for me.'

'You wouldn't marry me to give our baby a name.'

He hadn't meant to blurt that out. But the memories of what had happened back then had forced their way through the barriers he had put up against her ten years ago and spilled out in words.

The flush deepened to scarlet, staining her fair skin. 'But it turned out there was no baby, didn't it?'

He could sense the effort required to keep her voice on an even keel.

Towards the end of their second month together in Santorini Claudia had become uncharacteristically anxious and edgy. At first he'd assumed it was because she was worried—as he was—about what would happen after her vacation came to an end. Finally, clearly terrified of what his reaction would be, she'd told him her period was ten days late and she feared she might be pregnant.

Stefanos had immediately offered to marry her. Not out of honour, or because it had been the right thing to do, but because he had been desperately in love with her. He'd known he'd found 'The One'. He'd been dreading her going back to university in England. Now she wouldn't have to. She would stay in Greece with him. He'd been twenty—not too young to take on the responsibility. He'd wanted her…wanted the baby. He'd known he could give her everything she'd need.

She'd panicked. He still remembered her words, searing through his declaration of love and commitment, kicking it back in his teeth. *'I don't want to be a teenaged mum. I don't want to get married.'*

'A false alarm,' was all he said now. He'd been so naïve—believing that because he loved someone, she'd love him back with the same intensity. He'd had everything to offer her, but it hadn't been enough. *He* hadn't been enough.

'Yes,' she said.

Her period had come just as he'd thought he was making progress in convincing her of his love and sincerity, telling her how her life would be as the wife of the heir to billions. Her relief at what she'd called 'a lucky escape' had been palpable—in fact she'd done a little dance of joy on the deck of his yacht…the beautiful vintage racing yacht the *Daphne*, which his grandparents had gifted him for his eighteenth birthday. She'd expected he'd be as relieved as she was, and had been genuinely surprised when he'd expressed disappointment that there wouldn't be a baby.

He'd tried to convince her that even without a pregnancy he wanted to marry her. It hadn't been an option for her.

'Can't you see we're too young, Stefanos?'

She'd wanted to finish her degree, to have a career and see the world. He'd been obliged to prove himself in the family business, with working alongside his father all he'd been able to see on his horizon.

'Marriage, babies—all that would erase the future I want for myself.'

He'd felt erased. It had been a deep, abiding hurt that had prompted him to wipe away all contact with her. He'd vowed he would never again let a woman hurt him like that.

And here they were in the future. Having met only by chance. With not a lot to say to each other. Maybe what he'd taken for love had been about sex. Hot, passionate, exhilarating sex. They'd thought they'd discovered a secret no one else could possibly have discovered before them, revelling in the pleasures their bodies could give each other. He'd been in a constant state of arousal around her, crazy with want and a fierce desire to make her his.

In a cheap, white cotton dress—supposedly Greek, but actually made in India—that had showed off her long, elegant legs, and with a straw hat jammed on top of her salt-tangled bright hair she'd been sexy in a subtle, enticing way. She was just as desirable now—he couldn't deny it. That awful baggy T-shirt and leggings couldn't mask her slender figure, its curves subtle but more than enough to tantalise him. She had grown even more womanly and beautiful, though he preferred her hair long, tumbling down to her waist in a glorious copper fall.

Nothing had been the same after the pregnancy scare. They'd held themselves apart from each other. She'd been planning to stay with him in Santorini for as long as possible into September, before she had to return to Birmingham for the start of her second year at university. Instead, she'd lasted for just a few days of the awkwardness that had sprung up between them before she'd told him she'd changed her flight home.

Now she picked up the chunky tape dispenser, put it down on top of a box that was still only half sealed. Stefanos knew she was doing it to avoid his scrutiny. He realised his arms were still folded across his chest. He unfolded them and shoved his hands into the pockets of his trousers.

Finally she took a step towards him. 'Why did you ghost me? Cut off any means of getting in touch with you?'

'I told you that if we couldn't be together that was the end of it. I was—still am—an all-or-nothing guy.'

He'd been determined to protect himself against further hurt from her. Besides, he had never known a vacation romance that had lasted longer than the summer. She hadn't wanted to marry him—why drag out the pain?

'We talked about staying friends,' she said.

He shook his head. '*You* talked about staying friends. You didn't listen to what I was saying.'

'I didn't want to hear what you were saying. It...it was so hurtful.'

He'd been hurt too. He'd driven her to the small airport at Santorini in silence. Their farewell had been cool and stilted. When he'd got back to the boat he'd noticed that the straw hat she had worn all summer had slipped to the floor of the car and she'd left it behind. For a long time he'd held it close, and had felt as though his heart was being ripped out of his chest.

Now the dregs of past emotion choked his voice and he had to clear his throat to speak. 'I thought I'd made it very clear I wanted you as my lover, as my wife, as the mother of my children. Being a "friend" wouldn't have been enough for me.'

'We could have tried long-distance dating. I thought—'

'*All or nothing.* Where would you have seen the *all* in you living in England and me in Greece? You'd already knocked back the idea of a future with me.'

'Not a future. Just marriage. And children.'

'The things that were important to me.'

'I was left with the *nothing* and it was terrible.' She clutched her right hand—still in its work glove—to her chest. He wondered if she realised she was doing it.

Her voice hitched. 'That awful drive to the airport…as if we were strangers. I cried all the way through check-in and onto the plane. I cried until I didn't have a tear left. But I thought I'd at least be able to text you. Or talk to you on social media. But you blocked me every which way and all I had was that great big *nothing*.'

She drew in her breath with a big, anguished gulp that tore straight to his heart.

'It was the way it had to be,' he said.

For his own sanity if nothing else. Although seeing her distress now, still real after all this time, he realised he could have done it better. It had been immature—cruel, even—to handle it the way he had. He should at least have told her he intended to wipe her. But that was the way he'd been aged twenty.

'But you got over it?' she asked, her voice shaky.

'Eventually. Inevitably.'

She didn't meet his eyes. 'I… I did too.'

By the time he'd turned twenty-two he'd been married to Arina.

CHAPTER THREE

FOR SO LONG Claudia had suppressed the pain of losing Stefanos. Now being with him was bringing it back, and it was burning into her heart like drops of acid. She realised she was pushing against her own chest, as if to contain the agony of it, and she dropped her hand to her side.

She'd thought it would be nice—healing, even—to talk to him about the past, about where they both were now. Adult to adult. Laughing a little, perhaps, as they reminisced about their time together in Santorini. No pain. No anguish. Just a string of *Do you remembers?*

It wasn't working out like that. Since Kitty's wedding in February Claudia had found herself questioning the choices she'd made, the way she'd hedged her life in with constraints. The way she now found herself on her own and heading for thirty.

For the first time in years she'd thought about Stefanos and wondered if she had made the wrong decision back then. And now here he was. Unlocking the hurtful memories she'd fought so hard to block. And his memories of her were so obviously underscored with bitterness.

Who had hurt who the most?

She looked up to find his eyes on her, brown with intriguing flecks of green, filled not with accusation but with something she couldn't read. It made her feel even more self-conscious. The full force of her attraction to him hit her. Not to him then, but to him *now*. He was even more handsome as a man, that darker edge to him adding to his appeal.

At nineteen, in the depths of her anger at his inflexibility, she'd wanted to believe what her friends had told her: she shouldn't take it so badly…she'd meet another man…there were many more gorgeous guy pebbles on the beach. She *had* met other men, but no one had ever stirred her body and her heart the way Stefanos had.

Rehashing their painful parting with him, knowing how dismal her love-life had been ever since, realising she might have made a very big mistake ten years ago, was just too distressing. But it wasn't possible to go backwards in life. Here, now, ripping open wounds she'd thought had healed to barely discernible scars was too much to endure.

She couldn't do this.

'This isn't working out,' she said abruptly—too abruptly. But she was struggling to maintain her composure. She stripped off her other work glove. She wouldn't be needing it now. 'I'll call my other packer. Actually, I'll book two packers, to make up for the time I've wasted. Of course I won't charge for the extra person.'

'Good idea,' he said.

His instant agreement stung. Perversely, she'd wanted him to protest at her leaving. Her redhead's temperament sometimes made her speak before she'd fully thought things through. This time, though, she'd had little choice. She couldn't be put through the emotional wringer over events long past by a man who, it seemed, still had power to hurt her.

She picked up her mobile phone from where she'd put it down on the sleek cube of a coffee table. It was an effort to force her voice to sound businesslike and not reveal she was teetering on the edge of tears.

Thankfully, her two preferred packers were available to start ASAP.

She put down the phone and turned to Stefanos. 'I'll stay until I can confirm they're on their way.' Damn that note of shakiness in her voice. 'Then I'll be gone.'

He frowned. 'Gone where?'

'Back home. To another job. Just…gone.' She could hardly choke out the words.

Anywhere but here with him.

Her eyes darted around the room—to the ancient maps on the wall, that incredible urn… anywhere but at Stefanos.

He stepped towards her. 'Don't go, Claudia. Stay. Stay with me.'

Was she hearing things?

She was too shocked to reply.

'Let your people come in and finish the packing. But I'd like to spend some time with you. Talk about where life has taken you.'

'You mean fill in the ten-year gap?'

'As best we can.'

'Like…not exactly like friends, but…but friendly acquaintances?'

'Friendly acquaintances?' He was very serious. 'Something like that. Surely we've met by chance for a reason. We should take advantage of that. I think we'd both regret it if we let that chance slip by. It's unlikely we'll ever see each other again.'

'Perhaps… I… I never told you why I was so against—'

He put up his hand. 'No need for that. I can see that talking about the past upsets you.'

'There was hurt on both sides. Perhaps I didn't understand that at the time.'

'I can see I could have done things differently.'

She hesitated. Then, 'Yes. I'd like to take the chance to catch up.' She felt both relief and just the faintest stirring of excitement.

'Good,' he said. And he smiled. For the first time that morning he smiled.

That hadn't changed at all: his perfect white teeth—she'd used to tease him that he could model in a toothpaste commercial—the way his smile lit his eyes. It brought memories of *her* Stefanos flooding back and she couldn't stop looking at him, taking in every change and everything that remained the same.

He'd been such fun, but at the same time somehow more grown-up than her, even though there was only a year between them. Now he was quite the commanding presence. She'd used to tease him and laugh with him—now she didn't know that she would dare.

She indicated the room with a sweep of her hand. 'When my packers get here it won't be private.'

The last thing she wanted was her staff to overhear her personal conversation. Especially with a man as outstandingly handsome as Stefanos. She could only imagine the gossip swirling around the ranks of full-time staff and into the casuals who worked when they could fit it in around family obligations. She'd learned the hard way to keep her personal life private.

'We won't be here,' he said, the smile still lingering in his eyes. 'I don't know about you, but I'm in need of coffee.'

She smiled. 'Me too.'

He'd taught her to appreciate Greek coffee, *glykos*, which was strong and very sweet. She hadn't drunk it for ten years, but she had definitely become something of a caffeine addict.

'How long did you live here?' she asked.

'For a year.'

'Then I'm sure you know a good place for coffee.'

She could do this.

'I'm staying in a hotel nearby after the apartment is packed up,' he said. 'I fly to Athens tomorrow.'

Tomorrow he'd be gone. Claudia felt powered by a sudden sense of urgency—a kind of greed. She had to grab this chance to spend time with him, even if it stirred up old hurts. As he'd said, so matter-of-factly, there might never be another.

'Sensible idea,' she said. 'People often stay elsewhere during the disruption of packing for a move.'

'I could take you to the hotel for coffee.'

'I would like that,' she said.

He told her where the hotel was, and she realised it was an ornate nineteenth-century hotel, famous in Bloomsbury. She would have loved to see it. It was very posh. But not in trainers and leggings.

She looked down at her clothes in dismay. 'I'll have to change,' she said.

'You could get away with what you've got on,' he said wryly. 'No one seems to care what people wear.'

'*I* care,' she said firmly. Fortunately she had a change of clothes with her, as she had plans to catch up with Kitty after work. 'I can get changed before we go.'

'How long do we need to wait for your packers?'

'If you're happy for them to work without you being here we don't need to wait. Everything is straightforward. These two women are completely trustworthy. Your possessions will be in safe hands. And they can call me if they have any queries.'

'They're women?'

'Yes. That's the whole idea behind PWP. We—my partner Kitty and I—found people appreciated having women taking care of packing their possessions when moving house.' She put up her hand to forestall the comment she often got. 'That's not to say men can't do a brilliant job too. It's just we've built our business around helping people who prefer the female touch.'

'Yet you're called People Who Pack?'

'We originally called the business Ladies Who Pack, but we were criticised for being sexist.' She laughed. 'We worked freelance before we started the business, and we were always referred to as "those ladies who pack". But now we do have some very good men working for us as part of the team.'

'You're successful?'

'Yes. We were fortunate to get some good recommendations, and the publicity around my business partner Kitty marrying Sir Sebastian Delfont—who was our client—certainly gave us a boost. As a matter of fact...' She stopped herself.

'Yes?' he said.

She made a dismissive wave of her hand. 'You don't want to hear about it.'

'But I do. I'm intrigued.'

'I don't want to bore you.'

'From my memories of you, Claudia, you could never be boring,' he said.

His slow smile and narrowed eyes brought a new blush to her cheeks.

'We've had an approach from an investor who wants to talk about franchising opportunities,' she said.

'Are you interested?'

'We haven't had time to give it much thought. I like being in control…keeping standards high. But Kitty can't be as involved as she once was. She's become heavily involved in a charitable trust set up by Sebastian's grandmother. We might have to look at other options.'

'It's always wise to look for new opportunities.'

'Even when they might be a bit scary?' she said.

'Especially when they might be a bit scary,' he said. 'Accepting new challenges is how you grow.'

'You sound like quite the businessman, dispensing words of wisdom,' she said.

'It's in the blood—there's no escaping it,' he said with a wry smile.

Funny, she'd known him as the son of a billionaire, the grandson of a billionaire. Now he was undoubtedly a billionaire himself. And yet he'd always been just Stefanos to her, and that didn't seem to have changed.

'Give me a moment to get out of these clothes,' she said, immediately wishing she hadn't said that. When they'd been together that would have signalled something altogether different from going out for coffee. 'I mean, get changed…you know…put on different—'

Damn, why did that slow, lazy grin make her blush even hotter?

'I know exactly what you mean,' he said, and she felt his gaze follow her out of the room.

While Claudia was getting changed in the main bathroom, Stefanos gave the apartment a silent farewell. He had inherited it from his grandfather on his mother's side, and it had been both an investment and a family *pied-à-terre* for business trips to London. He'd often stayed here as a child, when he'd been taken to London on vacation to work on perfecting his English.

He'd had it gutted and refurbished to his own taste and moved in a year ago, for a year of living *by* himself and *for* himself, escaping from the trauma of his second marriage and finally being able to follow his interests in archaeology.

Now he had got everything he needed from his time here, and it was time for him to go back home. He would let the apartment. There was no point in having it sitting empty when it could be earning revenue.

All thoughts of the apartment or anything else flew away when Claudia walked back into the living room on a wafting scent of something sweet and feminine. She was wearing a multi-pleated skirt in an abstract print like large leopard spots, cinched around her narrow waist with a wide black belt, and a scoop-neck black top that emphasised her long neck and the curve of her breasts. She had a light black coat flung around her shoulders. Her hair was sleek and smooth, subtle make-up emphasised the blueness of her eyes, and her generous mouth was slicked with a soft red. She wore sheer black stockings, spiky heeled black shoes, and carried a large black tote bag.

He swallowed hard. 'You look…sensational,' he managed to choke out.

She was stylish, sophisticated, sexy…with the subtle sensuality that was as attractive now as it had been back then. So grown up—and yet he could still see the girl he'd loved in the woman she'd become. He had to force himself not to stare hungrily and take in every detail.

'Thank you,' she said. 'After wearing my work uniform so many hours of the week, I like to dress a little better when I'm not on duty.' She laughed. 'I'm not dressed like this to go home on the Tube. I'm meeting my friend and business partner Kitty for a drink this evening.'

She was going out to a bar… What man would be hitting on her there tonight? Every guy in the place, most likely. Surprised at the surge of un-warranted jealousy, he had to remind himself that Claudia was well and truly in his past. Such thoughts were quite out of order for a 'friendly acquaintance'.

A phone sounded from the small black handbag she had slung over her shoulder and she reached for it.

'The packers have texted to say they're on their way.'

'We should be on our way too,' he said.

The sooner he had her to himself, the better. This time he wanted to say goodbye to her on better terms than he had ten years ago.

CHAPTER FOUR

AS CLAUDIA WALKED side by side with Stefanos into the elaborate Victorian era hotel on Russell Square, with its multiple arches and turrets, she had a feeling she was entering an entirely different world—Stefanos's billionaire world of extreme wealth and privilege.

She was no stranger to luxury hotels—but as a member of staff not as a well-heeled guest. She knew from the attitude of the attentive staff who greeted them that she was in the company of a valued and generous client. She straightened her shoulders and stood a little taller, enjoying their discreet glances at her, knowing she looked good in her new skirt—a designer sale bargain.

The lobby was nothing short of magnificent, with mosaic floors, columns and ornate ceilings. Victorian excess at its finest with a modern update. She had to smile at the contrast to Stefanos's minimalist white apartment. Not the kind of hotel she'd thought he might choose to stay after his possessions had been packed. But it was nearby, and she remembered he had always been a practical kind of person.

They were ushered into the hotel café and seated at a small round table, inviting in its intimacy, overlooking Russell Square Gardens. Claudia passed on the offer of a pastry, delicious as they looked. Her stomach was too tied up in knots to handle anything other than a black coffee. It was just too surreal for words that she was sitting in a London hotel across a table from Stefanos and that the waiters obviously thought they were a couple.

Wrong, she wanted to tell them. We're just friendly acquaintances. Of course it wasn't true. She could pretend that was the case for the sake of civil conversation with Stefanos, but they were ex-lovers and she couldn't forget that—not even for a second. Because all she could think about was what it would be like to be in his arms again.

'I noticed you were inspecting the hotel with a critical eye,' he said. 'What's your verdict?'

'Was I that obvious?' she said. 'I thought I was being very discreet.'

'I could see,' he said.

He'd always said she wasn't good at hiding her feelings. Perhaps that was because he had known her so well he'd been able to read her face. They'd used to marvel that they felt as if they'd known each other for ever almost as soon as they'd met. But that was something too personal for her to remind him of—or for her to dwell on.

'My verdict is that they've done a great job bringing the splendidly ornate heritage of the hotel up to date,' she said. 'It's welcoming, not intimidating. And the staff are attentive and well trained—that's really important.'

'I stayed here while the apartment was being remodelled and thought it excellent. I'm pleased you agree.' He paused to take a sip of his coffee. 'Tell me where your hotel career took you. I remember you wanted to see the world.'

That was safe ground—as long as she avoided any mention of the last hotel where she'd worked. A romance with a colleague had backfired in the worst possible way, with her being accused of *his* fraudulent misdemeanours.

'After graduation, I started an internship in London. London credentials are good to have on the résumé.'

'I can believe that,' he said.

'Next was a stint in a wonderful hotel in Paris—my dream job in many ways as I'm fluent in French.'

'You have a flair for languages. I remember you picked up Greek very quickly.'

'Purely conversational,' she said, pleased that

he'd remembered. 'I never got the hang of the alphabet.'

'You were only there a few months.'

'Yes,' she said.

She felt the air was thick with flashes of memory of that time—most of them highly sensual. No wonder she'd never had time to learn the Greek alphabet. She'd been too busy making love with Stefanos. She had to press her knees together at the memory of the pleasure he had aroused in her.

Did he remember?

Was he feeling the same shivers of desire she did when she looked at him and thought about how perfect they'd been together?

'Did you ever work at a Greek hotel?' he asked.

Their eyes caught for a moment too long. 'No. I've never been back to Greece. Not after… Well, not after what happened with…with us.'

It would have been way, way too painful to be back in his country without him. For the rest of her life Greece would be associated with Stefanos and the hurt of their parting; she doubted she would ever visit Greece again.

'I see,' he said.

Did he really?

'My brother had moved to Australia. I went to Sydney to see him and meet his Aussie wife and kids and try my chances there. Sydney became my base—not just for working within Australia, but also New Zealand and Bali. I loved Sydney. At one stage I even thought of settling there.'

Until betrayal had sent her fleeing home to the UK.

She'd thought she'd met the second great love of her life, until she had discovered she'd been scammed. He was a good-looking Aussie, who had been her manager at a five-star city hotel and her lover—who had never told her he was married.

'Home is always a drawcard,' Stefanos said.

He was right. Home was a refuge. She missed her mother and the twin sisters who had wreaked such havoc in her teenage life. Her mother could be flighty, and overly dependent on a man, but Claudia knew she would always be there for her.

'Your turn now. Why two divorces?'

She was aching with curiosity. And couldn't help a stab of jealousy at the thought of him being with any woman other than her. One—two—he had loved enough to marry. Unreasonable and irrational, she knew, as she hadn't wanted to marry him. But it was impossible not to feel it.

His dark eyebrows rose. 'Even after ten years I think you know I won't be discussing that with you.'

'C'mon. Just a line or two,' she urged. 'You can't deny me that. Not after telling me you're divorced twice by age thirty.'

'As persistent as ever, I see.'

'Some things don't change.'

Was she flirting with him? She certainly didn't mean to. What would happen if she did? If she leaned across the table and took his hand. Whispered that she still wanted him.

Another shiver of desire ran through her.

'I'll tell you what you could easily find by looking me up on the internet,' he said. 'I married the daughter of a family friend when I was twenty-two.'

'That…that was not long after—'

'Classic rebound. That was what some said when we separated on our six-month wedding anniversary.'

'Oh, my gosh, I'm sorry,' she said, not sure what else she could say.

'We weren't suited,' he said, thin-lipped and dismissive.

'I hardly dare ask about the second.'

'Then don't. Here's a one-word answer—*liar.*'

'That sounds bad.'

'It was,' he said grimly. 'Please don't ask me for further details because they will not be forthcoming.' He put up his hand. 'And don't say sorry again.'

'Sorry—I mean, sorry for saying sorry. I won't say it again.'

'Good,' he said with a twitch of his lips, obviously failing in an effort not to smile. Somehow the half-smile was even sexier than his full-on smile.

She picked up her coffee and put it down again without drinking. 'Before you ask, I have nothing of any interest to impart about my personal life. The only thing of significance is that I fancied myself in love with someone and he turned out to be married. Needless to say it didn't end well.'

She forced her tone to be light-hearted, as if it were of no consequence, but of course it had been. Brad had implicated her in a fraud involving inflated contracts for supplies from companies owned by his wife's family that included kickbacks for him. She was still bruised from the fallout. And she was still paying off her legal fees.

'Now it's my turn to say—how did you put it?—no further details will be forthcoming.'

'And my turn not to say sorry?'

She laughed, and after a moment he joined in. Her heart nearly stopped at the sight of Stefanos laughing, his head thrown back. She heard the deep rumbling sound of it that she'd always found so infectious. It brought everything rushing back: their first kiss while watching the famous sunset at Oia, over the waters of the Santorini caldera. The first time they'd made love, later that night on the mahogany deck of his beautiful white-sailed yacht. And so many times after that, each time better than the last.

Had their lovemaking been as spectacular as she remembered? Another rush of desire ran through her. She couldn't meet Stefanos's eye in case he guessed—in that way he had—what she was thinking.

Two cups of coffee on top of what he'd already had for breakfast was all Stefanos could manage or he would be wired. But he wanted to prolong his time with Claudia. So he ordered a third. If he could keep her here a little longer he could suggest an early lunch. He wasn't ready for her to leave.

Claudia pushed her half-drunk coffee away from her. 'That's enough for me,' she said. 'Even though it's very good coffee.'

'I don't really want this third cup either,' he admitted.

He didn't know why he was so reluctant to say goodbye to her. Throughout those two cups of coffee he'd been trying not to think about how awesome he and this beautiful, sexy woman had been together in bed. How much he'd like to take her by the hand and lead her up to his room right now to see if it was still as good.

But it was about more than sex. He could only put it down to feeling so relaxed in her company. More relaxed than he'd felt with any woman in recent times. He and Claudia had known each other a long time ago—in a different life—and, while the relationship had run its course to a bitter ending, it had been good while it lasted. But it was long over. Now there were no expectations for anything else. There was just the undeniable pleasure of being with her.

He'd forgotten how the simplest things she said could make him laugh—not necessarily the words, but the way she delivered them. He wondered if she felt in any way the same, because her eyes had lost some of that haunted look. There hadn't been a lot of laughter in his life in recent years…perhaps it had been the same for her.

She pushed her chair back from the table, inadvertently brushing his legs with hers as she did so. She didn't seem to notice, whereas to him the slight contact was like a jolt of electricity.

He wanted her.

'I'm not used to sitting for long these days,' she said. 'I'd really like to have a look around the hotel. You're a guest here—what if you gave me a guided tour?'

'I don't know about a guided tour, but I can

certainly walk around with you. I lived here for a few weeks, so I know it fairly well.'

He would have to be very careful to maintain a distance between them. And keep his eyes off the swell of her breasts revealed by the low neckline of her top.

There were some splendid public areas of the hotel, and as they walked through them together he noted her professional enthusiasm. She seemed to know her stuff when it came to hotels. So why was she packing boxes when her earlier life had been spent in the pursuit of a career in hospitality? He still hadn't got a satisfactory answer.

As they made their way to one of the informal sitting rooms they encountered a large catering trolley, blocking the turn of the corridor. The staff member apologised and started to pull the trolley backwards, away from them.

'No, no, it's okay,' Claudia said, no doubt feeling empathy for the guy as former hotel staff herself, or just because she was well-mannered and considerate. 'We can squeeze by—can't we, Stefanos?' She looked up at him.

He looked at the tight space. Did she realise just how tight it was? Only if they squeezed themselves up against each other could the trolley get by.

'Of course,' he said, not able to hide his anticipation.

He found himself hard up against her, her hips against his, her breasts against his chest, their arms tight by their sides. It was the closest he had been to her in ten years.

It seemed a very long moment as the trolley trundled by them. Claudia looked up at him, cheeks flushed, her pupils so huge they virtually eclipsed the blue of her eyes. He could feel her nipples pebble…no doubt she could feel his arousal. Her breathing was coming a little harder and he fought to control his.

They stood close for a moment too long before she pulled away from him. She pushed her hair back from her face when she didn't really need to do so, and he remembered it was something she did when she was nervous.

'Er… I'd love to see that sitting room—the one with the palm trees you mentioned. That you thought I'd like.' She spoke way too fast and didn't meet his eyes.

When they got to the room she made too many observations, praised it too lavishly. Made sure she kept a non-touching distance away from him. Then she spluttered to a stop. At last she looked up at him. Took a deep breath that made her breasts rise enticingly.

'I'd love to see inside the bedrooms,' she said. 'Would it be pushing our friendly acquaintance-ship too far to ask to see yours?'

Her blue eyes were innocent of guile, yet he could not say the same of himself. *Claudia. His bedroom.* He wasn't thinking about the furnishings.

He nodded, cleared his throat. 'I'm staying in the penthouse.'

She smiled a slow smile. He wasn't sure what to make of it—which made it all the more exciting.

'Of course you are,' she said. 'Are you sure you don't mind? I wouldn't be invading your privacy?'

'I don't mind at all.'

Inwardly he groaned. He hoped he was reading her right.

Claudia in his bedroom.

If he hadn't read her right it would be a huge effort of will to keep his mind on anything but how utterly desirable he still found her.

CHAPTER FIVE

CLAUDIA DIDN'T REGISTER much about the penthouse suite except the enormous, contemporary-style four-poster bed. She didn't give a flying fig about what the room looked like—how elegantly it was furnished, the panelling on the walls. She tossed her coat on a chair and didn't notice when it slid to the thickly carpeted floor. All her senses were taken up with Stefanos and how much she had wanted him back then…

How much she wanted him now.

He'd opened the door to usher her through ahead of him. Now he stood facing her, with the closed door behind him, framing him. So big, so tall, so damned *sexy.* He didn't say a word. He didn't have to. Everything he might need to say was in his eyes, and she was sure he saw the same message in hers.

He took a step towards her.

At the same time she took two steps towards him.

Then she was in his arms.

At last.

She suppressed a sob of relief that he seemed to want this too.

He felt the same as he had the last time they'd been this close in an embrace, yet not quite the same. His chest was broader, more muscular, and his arms around her were more powerful. He hadn't worked out back then—he hadn't needed to. He'd got all the exercise he needed from working on the *Daphne*, swimming, and bedroom athletics with her.

She breathed in the familiar scent of him. It wasn't a cologne or a shampoo—it was *him*, and it hadn't changed at all. With his scent came a flood of memories, intoxicating and arousing. She looked up at him, intently taking in his face, so familiar and yet so unfamiliar. Was that tiny scar above his thick black eyebrow new? Or had she forgotten it over the space of ten years?

She rose on tiptoe at the same time as he dipped his head and their lips met in a kiss. The kiss was uncertain at first—a kiss between strangers who had once been intimate and were now tentative with each other. It was exciting, for sure, but part of her held back, analysing how she was feeling about this first kiss after such a long time. There was something different from all the countless kisses they'd shared before. The beard. That was what it was. Back then he'd been clean-shaven. She liked the difference. The brush of his beard on her skin was like an erotic tickle—an extra dimension of sensation.

The analysis lasted for mere seconds before their kiss quickly escalated to become hungry, urgent, demanding. Her heart raced, her breath came short, and a sudden rush of desire over-whelmed her. He pulled her tighter and pressed her body to his, breasts to solid chest, hips to the hardness of his thighs. He slid his hands down the side of her breasts, her waist. She realised he was remembering her body—her shape, her skin, her reactions. His hands felt good—they always had. Her nipples were so hard they ached, and when he reached down to cup her bottom she gasped in surprise, pleasure and arousal.

Impatiently she tugged his shirt from his trou-sers, so she could slide her hands up to splay them across the warmth and strength of his chest. In response, he walked her backwards to-wards the bed, each of them frantically attempt-ing to divest the other of clothing. She got as far as unbuckling his belt, and he removed her wide belt, before they fell onto the bed, facing each other. He pushed up her top to caress her breasts until she thought she would come just from the sheer pleasure of it. Her body remembered his, all right. He slid his hands up under her skirt to tug down her stockings, pull her lacy panties to one side. His intimate touch with skilled, knowing fingers was sheer ecstasy. He had always known exactly how to arouse her.

As they lay there, facing each other on the bed, he broke away from the kiss, took his hand from her. 'Is this what you want?' His voice was hoarse, his breath coming in great, ragged gulps. 'If not, say so now.'

'Yes…' she managed to get out in a suddenly husky voice. 'Yes. Don't stop. I want it. I want *you*.' She pulled him back to her. *'Now.'*

Hands unsteady with haste, she unzipped his trousers and pushed them down past his hips over strong thighs, following them with his boxers. She circled his erection with her hand. *That* hadn't changed, she thought, as she trembled in anticipation of the pleasure she knew he could give her.

He bunched her skirt up above her hips, yanked down her stockings to her ankles, tore her lacy panties in his haste to remove them. No need to undress further. She bucked her hips towards him, writhing with impatience.

'Protection,' he said hoarsely, and he broke away to reach for a small satchel on the nightstand.

Thank heavens he'd remembered, she thought. She was so on fire for him, so desperate for him to enter her, she might not have thought about protection, and that would have undone ten years of caution against her fear of pregnancy.

Protection in place, she pulled him down to her. 'I'm ready for you. *Please.*'

There was a distinct whimper in her voice. She didn't care if she sounded as if she was begging. She *was* begging. She wanted him—*needed* him. And it had been so long. She couldn't wait a second more.

When he pushed inside her, filling her, thrusting, she moaned in her intense pleasure and then almost immediately convulsed around him in a mind-blowing orgasm that had her crying out his name. *'Stefanos!'* No one had ever made her feel the way he did—that intensity of sensation, that power.

As she came down from the heights he held her close. Then he continued his steady, rhythmical possession of her body until she came again, in an intense rush of pleasure, accompanied by his great shout of release. They'd practised their timing back then—who knew a simultaneous orgasm would still be so effortless for them now?

She fell back onto the bed, exhilarated, laughing, face flushed. She looked down at her skirt, all bunched up above her waist, her top rucked up above her bra—heck, she still had her shoes on. But then so did he...

She looked up at him. His eyes were dilated,

his expression unreadable. He had closed his eyes at the moment of climax. Back then in Santorini they had always looked into each other's eyes—trying, he'd said, to see inside each other's soul.

'That was fast and furious,' she said. She reached up and stroked her fingers down his cheek. Her voice hitched. 'And utterly wonderful. Thank you.'

He caught her hand and kissed her fingers one by one. 'I haven't finished with you yet,' he said, in a deep, determined voice that sent more shivers of anticipation down her spine.

'I like the sound of that,' she murmured.

Slowly he divested her of her top, then her bra, and pinned her hands above her head with one hand while kissing her breasts, tonguing one nipple while he rolled the other between thumb and finger. The pleasure was almost painful.

Just as she was about to implore him to stop—it was simply too pleasurable to bear—he moved down, kissing a path to the top of her skirt, the soft brush of his beard adding to her rising excitement. He found the zipper and soon she was only in her torn black lace panties. He took the remnants of those in his teeth and smoothed them down over her thighs, kissing every inch of her along the way, bringing her yet again almost to the point of orgasm.

'I like these shoes,' he said. 'You look very

sexy in them and nothing else. But I'd prefer the nothing else.'

He took off her spike heel slingbacks, caressing her toes and the arch of each foot as he did so until, squirming with ticklish laughter, she had to pull them away. It was silly that amid all this thrilling pleasure she felt glad she'd had a pedicure only two days before and that her legs were waxed.

She sat up and pushed him by his shoulders, down onto his back. 'This is a little one-sided, isn't it?' she said, kneeling over him, dominating him. 'We have to remedy that. Now it's my turn to torture you.'

It was an old game between them—one she hadn't given thought to for years. But here he was again, under her sensual control, and she thrilled to the power of it. She loved the way he narrowed his eyes in anticipation as he raised his arms in surrender to her wishes.

Claudia unbuttoned his shirt and stripped it off him, tossing it dramatically to the floor. Memories of what had pleased him back then flooded her. Would she still please him now? Teasingly, she kissed him all over his face—on his eyelids, on his nose, on the corners of his mouth. But she wouldn't let him capture her mouth in a kiss— that was part of the torture.

She kissed behind his ears, the hollows of his

throat, the tops of his arms—which seemed to particularly please him—and across his chest. She kissed, nibbled and sucked a pathway down his belly, loving the way his muscles went rigid and he groaned at her teasing touch. She flirted briefly with his bold erection—until he asked her to stop unless she wanted the game to end right there and then. So she moved down his legs to take off his shoes and tug off his trousers.

She surveyed his gloriously naked body, the smooth olive skin with a dusting of dark hair in all the right places. His defined musculature was like a statue of one of the most perfect Greek gods from ancient times.

'Impressive,' she sighed, aroused just by the sight of him. 'Although I'm not sure about the socks-only look… They really have to go.'

He laughed and pulled her into his arms. This time their lovemaking was slow and sensual and even more satisfying—for him as much for her, she hoped.

Sated, she drowsed, wrapped in his arms. Although as she drifted off the thought persisted: again, he hadn't looked into her eyes as he climaxed. Maybe that lack of intimate communication was the difference between two people deeply in love—as they had once been—and two friendly acquaintances slaking their sexual appetites with each other.

* * *

Stefanos, propped on one elbow, watched Claudia as she slept. The late-morning May sunshine filtered through the curtains, illuminating the tumble of her auburn hair with copper glints where it spread against the white of the bed linen.

Her darkened eyelashes fluttered—was she dreaming? Dreaming of *him*?

He could see the delicate bluish-green veins under the translucent skin around her closed eyes. One long, slender leg rested over his. Her skin was strikingly pale against his with its darker olive tone. Her colouring made her look fragile, but he knew she had a strength that belied her appearance. Her body was toned, with sleek muscles. And there was nothing fragile about her sensual responses. Just like in their long-ago past, she matched him for sexual appetite.

Inwardly, he sighed. After they'd broken up he had never again experienced sex such as he'd shared with her. He'd grown to realise how very rare that level of connection was. Today their bodies had read other's wants as if ten years had never passed.

But great sex wasn't enough.

She smiled in her sleep—just a faint upturning of her lovely mouth, swollen from his kisses. Definitely dreaming of him, he thought.

Back then, he had often watched her like this as she slept, scarcely able to believe that she was his. His hadn't been an adolescent love. He had loved her with a man's heart and soul, and had known with a passionate certainty that he wanted to spend his life with her. He had wanted a child with her, to make a family with her, to share his wealth, his heart, *everything* with her.

Her rejection of him had hardened his heart against her and led him to two disastrous marriages. But right now, in the afterglow of great sex, he was inclined to think more kindly of her. After all, she'd only been nineteen. Now, in spite of their obvious physical compatibility, it was too late for them to try again. Their time with each other had come and gone. He was a different person now: distrustful, wary, and cynical when it came to women and their motives.

He'd been in so much pain over his loss of Claudia it had made him vulnerable—too ready to prove she wasn't the only woman he could love. Along had come his mother's goddaughter Arina, from another mega-wealthy Greek shipping family, newly graduated with a degree in marketing and doing an internship at Adrastos Shipping. Their match had been actively encouraged by both sets of parents. In fact there'd been an ongoing family joke that they, born six months apart, had been betrothed at birth.

Arina had grown into a beauty—petite, black-haired, with soulful brown eyes. The complete opposite, in fact, to Claudia. She was smart, sweet and kind. If anything, something of a people-pleaser—but that hadn't mattered when he was the person she was pleasing.

In his heart, Stefanos had known he hadn't felt for her what he'd felt for Claudia. But that kind of love only led to heartbreak and loss.

Their families had been delighted when he'd proposed after three months of dating, having convinced himself that Arina was exactly what he needed, and they'd had a big wedding in the cathedral in Athens, both aged twenty-two. Later, he'd realised that had been the happiest day of their entire marriage.

Their wedding night hadn't been a great success. She'd been a nervous virgin and shrunk away from him. And by the time their six-month wedding anniversary had rolled around the marriage had become sexless. That had been the day when Arina, in her kindest, sweetest voice, had told him she was leaving him.

She had fallen in love with someone else— had been in love with her for years, in fact, but unable to admit it. The chief bridesmaid at their wedding. Arina had been unable to deny her sexuality any longer—although she had tried to, for her conservative family's sake. She had apologised to Stefanos over and over. She cared about him, but she simply wasn't sexually attracted to him. He had told her there was nothing to forgive. That she had to stop pleasing other people instead of herself.

Their divorce hadn't stopped him liking her, and they had since maintained a genuine if somewhat distant friendship, but he admitted, if only to himself, how battered and bruised he had been by the experience of his one-sided marriage. Not so much because he had been rejected in favour of a woman—which had struck deeply at his masculinity and his pride as a Greek male even though he knew he shouldn't have let it— but rather it was her dishonesty and deception that had wounded him. She had lied to him from the start.

He'd been happy for Arina that she had found true love. But he'd been too scarred to look for it himself. How could he trust another woman to be what she said she was? Why hadn't he realised?

He had maintained that distrust but somehow, five years later, Tiana had sneaked under his defences. Perhaps it had been because at first she'd reminded him a little of Claudia—although her red hair had been dyed and her forthrightness had been fake too. But she'd been glamorous, exciting, not looking for anything from him but a good time and a supply of expensive gifts of jewellery with which he had obliged her. There was no emotional investment required in a diamond bracelet.

However non-stop fun had palled after a while. Tiana had cleverly read his mood and quietly confessed that all she really wanted was to settle down and have a family. He'd been charmed by her 'honesty'. Although the truth was that he'd been suckered by a mistress of the art.

Now, Claudia stirred in her sleep and opened her eyes, smiling when she saw him. She was so beautiful—everything he'd once wanted in a woman. But it was too late for him and her.

Too late, too late.

The refrain ran through his head as he forced a smile in return.

CHAPTER SIX

CLAUDIA OPENED HER eyes to see Stefanos lying beside her. Naked. She was naked too. In a hotel bed, in the late morning, in central London.

So it hadn't been a dream.

Surprisingly, she didn't feel awkward. What had happened between them had been entirely consensual and very, very good. Nevertheless, she pulled the linen sheet up above her breasts to cover her nakedness, and in doing so covered his.

He smiled at her, but the smile didn't quite reach his eyes. That was okay. He probably felt awkward. It was a potentially awkward situation. Who knew? Perhaps he expected her to hop out of bed, thank him and leave. They weren't really 'friendly acquaintances'—more like strangers. And she didn't have any expectations that there would be any more than this between them. They were very different people from those they'd been back then.

Back on the *Daphne* in Santorini, even after

she'd found out what the surname Adrastos stood for in Greece, they'd been equals. Her in a swimsuit, he in board shorts, in the blue waters that had belonged to everyone. Now they moved in very different worlds, and faced those worlds from very different perspectives.

His apartment, for instance, was no doubt just one dwelling in a portfolio of luxury properties. Whereas she was living in a rented maisonette in Hammersmith, building up her savings so she could buy a place of her own. What made for great communication in bed didn't necessarily translate to the world outside the bedroom.

'The sex was…unexpected,' she said.

He raised a dark eyebrow. 'Was it really? I was thinking about sex from the moment I first saw you.'

That sensual edge to his voice made her quiver every time.

'Perhaps I was too,' she admitted. 'When I first saw you, I mean.' Standing there in the doorway…his hostility adding an extra edge to his dark good looks.

He grinned, and there was a flash of the carefree young Stefanos she had loved.

'This…our lovemaking…completes things for me,' she said.

'You mean climax-wise?' he said with a lazy smile.

She smiled back. 'That too. But that was always good with you. What I meant was, we never had a "last time" together before I left Santorini.'

'We didn't,' he said.

In fact they'd scarcely been speaking.

'The pregnancy scare changed everything, didn't it? We didn't make love again after I... confessed my fears. Later I tried to remember when exactly we'd last been together and I couldn't.'

She'd been inexplicably saddened by that.

'Now you have closure?' he said. 'Is that what you mean?'

She frowned. 'Yes... No. I'm not sure if that's it, exactly. But closure is near enough.'

What she was trying to say was that she'd been left with a deeply buried unresolved longing for him. And now that had been resolved.

'Good,' he said.

She sat up to lean against the lavishly padded headboard. She found it difficult to meet his eye.

'Talking about back then—and before we say goodbye again—I... I want to tell you why I behaved the way I did when we...when we broke up.'

He sat up too, the sheets rucked around his hips. 'I thought we weren't going to go over the past.'

'I think I need to—for the closure thing, I mean.'

'I don't need closure,' he said. 'It was a long time ago. It's not possible to step twice into the same river, as we say in Greece.'

'Like we say water under the bridge—I get it. But can you humour me?'

To his credit, he didn't show any sign of impatience. 'If it's that important to you,' he said.

She realised she was clutching the sheet between her fingers and released her grip. 'You must have thought it unusual that I was so anti-marriage and anti-babies when most people hope for that sometime in their futures.'

'Yes,' he said. 'I'm an only child. I always knew I wanted one day to have a family with more than one child.'

And he'd made that so very clear to her at the time. It wasn't just that he'd been trying to be honourable, she realised, even at the age of twenty he had been ready to start a family. She hadn't.

'Do you remember I told you my father died when I was fifteen?' she said.

He nodded. 'I remember feeling sad for you. And now I've lost my own father I can appreciate even more how you must have felt.'

Even now, after all this time, she felt tears threaten when she thought about her beloved dad.

'He and my mother managed a pub—had done for many years. He died in an accident. A careless truck driver hadn't properly secured a load of wooden barrels of beer he was delivering. My father went to help unload and…and was hit when they suddenly rolled off the truck.'

Stefanos swore under his breath in Greek. 'A terrible accident.'

'Both terrible and tragic. His death triggered massive change in my life. For one thing we lived "above the shop", and we lost our home when the chain who owned the pub put in new managers. It was a huge wrench for me. I loved the pub…the visitors from around the world. I offered to step up and manage it myself, but of course they laughed at me.'

Stefanos smiled. 'You were fifteen.'

She managed a watery smile. 'I know… But I still think I could have done it. I'd tagged along after my father since I was a child.'

'Apart from the fact you were underage and not even allowed to drink at a licensed premises let alone run it.'

'All that,' she said with a sigh. 'My mother wasn't trained to take over the pub's management and nor did she want to. She'd been very happy to support Dad in everything he wanted to do, but her work at the pub was mainly behind the bar and in the restaurant—not management.'

'And she was a mother.'

'Yes. To me and my half-brother, who's five years older than me. He's from Dad's first marriage. His wife died when Mark was only a toddler. Mum was a good mother—still is. But most of all she was a wife. She went to pieces when Dad died. And I… I didn't know how to help her.'

'That must have tough for you.'

'It was. I was dealing with my own grief. It was a bad age to lose him.'

'Any age is a bad age to lose your father,' he said.

She put out her hand and laid it over his. 'I know. You must still be grieving. And your mother, too.'

Wordlessly, he nodded. She took away her hand. Even though they'd shared every intimacy a man and woman could share in the last few hours, she didn't want to appear presumptuous.

'My mum didn't seem to be able to function without a man in her life,' she said.

'What about your brother?'

'He was ready to help as much as he could, but there wasn't much he could do. Mum had been well-compensated by the pub company, as Dad had died while at work due to negligence, but we moved in with my grandparents—his parents—who didn't live far away. My mum was lost without a man in her life. Six months after Dad died she started dating a man who'd used to stay at the pub on business trips. He'd been friendly with both her and Dad.'

'That seems quick…'

'I thought so too. I resented the heck out of him. And you can imagine what my grandparents— Dad's parents—thought.'

'What was he like?'

'Nice enough. But he wasn't my dad. My dad had adored my mother. He would have been horrified that she found someone to replace him so quickly.'

'Or glad she'd found someone to care for her?' Stefanos said slowly. 'My mother is very lonely as a widow, despite her friends and family.'

'There is that…' Claudia said, somewhat grudgingly, not wanting to admit she might have been wrong about something so fundamental. 'I don't know how serious it was, or whether they were planning to get married. But they'd been together for less than six months when my mother fell pregnant.'

Stefanos's dark eyebrows rose. 'That must have been a shock. How did you feel about that?'

'Can you imagine how embarrassing it was for a sixteen-year-old to have a pregnant forty-year-old mother?'

'Had they planned it?'

She shuddered in remembered distaste. 'I thought it was kind of icky that she was having sex at her age, so I didn't ask. But Mum said it was an accident, that she'd believed she was too old to get pregnant.'

'Did you believe that?'

'I did. She'd finally gone back to the career she'd had before she gave it up to work with Dad. She'd been a veterinary nurse and had always told us how much she loved it and missed it. After Dad died she updated her qualifications and resumed her career—only to have to give it up again.'

'And the father?'

'He married her.' She paused. 'I rather think he thought he'd been trapped. Mum was fun and outgoing—always good for a laugh. I don't think he counted on a baby coming along to deflect her focus from him. It got even more complicated when they discovered she was having twins.'

'I remember you said you had twin sisters. You were very fond of them.'

'I was. I am. I love them. Trouble was, my stepfather was in IT and travelled a lot for work. He was often away when the twins were babies. And they were a lot of work. Mum couldn't handle them on her own. She certainly couldn't work in the career she'd finally returned to.'

'I'm beginning to see what you're getting at.'

Could anyone really imagine what it had been like? They'd have had to be there in that small house they'd all moved into as 'a family'.

'Yep, those babies really restricted my mother's life at a time when she hadn't expected that. And good old big sister was the live-in babysitter. Can you imagine studying for exams while looking after two babies? Or having to say no to a date with your first crush? I loved the twins, and I loved my mother—of course I did. But I sometimes felt I was going through a kind of teenage mum hell. It made me realise how much worse it would be if you actually were a teenage mum and unable to hand them back, like I did when my babysitting shifts were done.'

'What about their father?'

'I was too resentful of him for trying to take my father's place and for putting us all in that position by getting my mum pregnant to think too much about him. He simply wasn't significant for me. But when the twins got a little older and could call him Dadda he seemed to bond with them. He got a new job that kept him off the road and he moved his little family to Swindon, where they still live. I stayed with my grandparents in Devon to finish school. By the time I met you I'd finished my first year of uni. I was living away from home and felt as if I had been let off the leash.'

Stefanos slowly shook his head. 'Why didn't you tell me all this back then?'

'I didn't want to talk to anyone about all that— even you. I didn't want to be someone's daughter or stepdaughter or even half-sister. I was totally intent on forging my own identity. But perhaps I should have told you. Because then you might have seen why I was so horrified at the prospect of not only being a teenage mum, but of being dependent on a man and losing the career I so desperately wanted.'

He was silent for a long beat. 'It might have helped me understand why you reacted so vehemently against marriage to me...baby or no baby.'

'In hindsight, I should have told you. But then you might have wondered why I had kept it from you—given you an edited version of my life in the UK. Somehow in Santorini I wanted to leave all that behind. Not to talk to anyone about my family situation. To just be me—Claudia—with my past behind me and the future I'd planned for myself ahead.'

'I see,' he said.

Did he? Could he? Because, looking back, even she found it difficult to understand. Why, when she'd been so in love with him, hadn't she shared such an important part of her life?

There wasn't really any more to tell. Perhaps there were questions Stefanos might have asked...answers she might have given him. Perhaps she might have had the opportunity to tell him that she hadn't changed her stance on marriage since then. But Room Service were at the door.

'While you were asleep I ordered us some lunch,' he said. 'I thought we might be hungry.'

'After all that exercise, you mean?' she said.

The smile in his eyes told her he knew exactly the kind of exercise she meant.

He'd been right—she was hungry. Claudia sat opposite Stefanos at the round table in the dining area of his suite. They were both dressed in the lush black robes supplied by the hotel. He looked so good in black, with his dark hair and that green glint in his eyes, his sensual mouth... Even hotter than he'd been at twenty and just as energetic, she thought, with a secret, satisfied smile.

He'd ordered four separate meals to give her a choice. Such extravagance—yet he didn't seem to think it was an unusual thing to do. The room service waiter certainly hadn't blinked as he'd explained all four dishes.

'I remember you like healthy food,' Stefanos said.

Oddly, for someone who'd wanted a career

in hospitality back then, she didn't remember what he'd liked to eat. She'd loved the traditional Greek meals they'd shared—not just in the town restaurants but in the out-of-the-way tavernas he'd taken her to on the *Daphne*, where the vegetables on the menu had been grown in the garden behind and the cheese had been made with milk from the owner's goats. Surely, as a billionaire's son, he had had grander tastes than that.

Now, she chose poached chicken with a tarragon yogurt sauce and salad; he went for salmon. He ate with gusto, but her appetite deserted her after a few mouthfuls and she put down her fork. This was beginning to feel awkward. Too much like a date when it wasn't that at all. She almost wished she would be saved by a phone call, but she'd turned off her phone after a quick text to Kitty asking her to look after her clients for that afternoon. Kitty would no doubt call the two packers now working in Stefanos's apartment to check all was well. She would be aching with curiosity about the reason Claudia had asked them to take over.

'Shall we meet here for lunch the next time I'm in London?' Stefanos said.

Next time? Claudia was so shocked to hear him mention a 'next time' she couldn't find the words to answer. She had assumed this would be the only time she shared with him before they went their separate ways.

'Th-that would be nice,' she finally managed to stutter. She looked up at him. 'I mean to have lunch in the restaurant…not in your bedroom.'

Wonderful as this reunion had been, she had no intention of being his booty call in London.

His eyes met hers, clear and direct. 'That's what I meant too,' he said.

'Not that I haven't loved every minute with you. But…'

'We've both found closure,' he said smoothly.

Neither of them had voiced it, but she sensed his bitterness about her refusing to marry him still lingered—might always linger. Might he even, deep down, blame her for his two marriages that had ended in divorce? He'd used to tell her that vengeance was a big thing in Greece because of all the vengeful Greek gods of mythology. There was definitely now a darker edge to that beautiful, sunny-natured boy she'd loved that long-ago summer.

'Today was perfect. I wouldn't want to risk ruining it by…by repeating it,' she said.

Spending this time with him had reminded her of just how good they'd been together in bed, but it had been about sex, not love. And sex without love had never been on her personal agenda.

'My thoughts precisely,' he said. 'You can't go backwards in life.'

'Or step in the same river twice, as you said.'

'Exactly.'

'We often did think the same thing,' she said, with a short, forced laugh.

Except about the really important issues, like marriage and children. But who could have blamed her for not having them at the front of mind at the age of nineteen?

'There's just one thing I'd like to ask you.'

'Go ahead,' he said.

'You're not cheating on anyone with me today?'

His shocked expression gave her his answer even before he replied. 'I told you I was single and I meant that I was single—no ties.' He paused. 'I've had more than my share of entanglement since we last met...' The mouth that had so recently been kissing her was set in a grim line. 'But I'm not looking for marriage number three—which means no relationships that might give a woman the wrong idea, or any kind of expectations.'

'I see,' she said. That no doubt included her. 'I ask because I... I think I told you I had a bad experience with someone who didn't tell me he was married. I inadvertently hurt his wife and I... I was distressed about that.'

The expression on Stefanos's face flitted from surprise, to exasperation, to a quickly masked fondness and back to exasperation. 'Why do you have to be so damn *nice*, Claudia?'

'Am I? I try to do the right thing by people, but I've never thought of myself as being particularly *nice*.'

'Well, you were back then, and it appears you still are now.'

Had he really thought that? She remembered that grim journey to the airport...the way he had ghosted her. The way she hadn't told him the full story about why she didn't want marriage because she'd been so determined to preserve the image of herself she had created.

'I'm glad you think so,' she said. She took a deep breath. 'I'm glad we met inadvertently, and I'm glad about...about that.'

She waved her hand in the direction of the bedroom...the bed with its tangle of linen, the scent of their lovemaking. His scent was still on her, and she was in no rush to wash it off. She'd shower when she got home.

'Me too,' he said.

'Do you plan to come to London often?'

'Occasionally. I've had a year in London and now there are things in Athens that need my attention. But there are archaeologists here I want to keep in touch with. I'll be sure to look you up when I visit.'

His words were perfectly pleasant—matter-of-fact, almost. As if they really were friendly acquaintances, not a man and a woman who had made passionate love all morning, intimately explored each other's bodies, and brought each other to the pinnacle of pleasure. She swallowed hard against a pang of hurt that he didn't appear to have seen anything special in the gloriously sensual time they'd spent together.

'I'd like that.'

She pushed her chair away from the table, took a deep breath. She couldn't let him see that at that moment she yearned for something more.

'It won't be easy to say goodbye, so I'm not going to drag it out. I'll find my clothes and go.'

'You don't want to finish your lunch?'

She shook her head. There was no point in pro-longing this. If she didn't go she just might be silly and ask if he was sure the grown-up Stefanos and Claudia couldn't have a casual relationship... a friendship, even. She couldn't risk it. Because it wouldn't work. Not for her and nor, she sus-pected, for him. He was a self-confessed all-or-nothing guy—she was a woman who had never entertained the emotional risk of casual sex. Es-pecially with a man who had the potential to shat-ter her heart. Again.

She found her clothes where he'd flung them, on the floor next to the bed, and her shoes heels-up at the end. The torn panties were wrapped up in the sheets. She tucked them in her tote bag. Somehow she couldn't bring herself to put them in the wastepaper bin. It was awful for hotel staff to have to clear up after guests' sexual shenanigans—and, besides, it was kind of sexy the way Stefanos had torn them off her. Quite one of the highlights of the morning.

Dressed, she peered in the mirror. Hair dishevelled, mascara smeared around her eyes, lips swollen with the lipstick all kissed off, beard rash around her neck… She looked like a woman who had spent the morning in bed with her lover. Not her lover, she reminded herself. Her *former* lover, a *long-ago* lover, who still knew how to press her buttons and with whom she had managed to put some old hurts to rest. She couldn't forget that.

My God, he was gorgeous, though, and she had to stamp, crush, pound into the ground any lingering thoughts of *what if?* There would only be this morning for them, and she had to disengage with any wishful imaginings that there might be more.

She picked up her tote bag. She couldn't catch the tube looking like this. She would splurge on a taxi home and repair the damage before her catch-up with Kitty.

Stefanos was still sitting at the table, his meal unfinished. He had obviously not eaten a bite since she'd left the room. Seeing her, he immediately got up from the chair.

'You're ready,' he said slowly.

'Yes.' She covered the few steps between them. 'Stefanos,' she said. 'Thank you.'

'It is I who should be thanking you.'

'Let's thank each other, then,' she said.

He pulled her to him in a hug. The time for passionate kisses had passed. For what seemed like a long time she stood in the circle of his arms, with her head nestled against his shoulder. How secure and safe she felt there. But it was an illusion. She suspected this encounter with her first love would soon begin to seem like a dream.

She pulled back and looked up into his face. His eyes were dark and unreadable. 'I said I was curious about what kind of a man you'd grown up to be. I… I'm glad to see you're such a wonderful man. I hope everything works out for you when you get home.' She paused, drinking in his dark good looks for the last time. Then, 'Goodbye, Stefanos, *yiasou*.'

'*Yiasou*, Claudia,' he echoed, his voice hoarse.

She planted a kiss on his cheek, turned on her heel, picked up her tote bag and headed to the door without turning back. She could not let him see that her eyes were smarting with tears.

CHAPTER SEVEN

CLAUDIA HAD PLENTY of time to hail a taxi and get home to her maisonette in Hammersmith, shower, change, and then meet her friend at the Chelsea mansion on Cheyne Walk, overlooking the Thames, that Lady Kitty now called home. Sebastian was out of town on business, and they'd planned a girls night in.

Kitty greeted her with a hug. 'You look… glowing,' she said. 'What's responsible for that?' She narrowed her eyes. 'Or *who*? Has this got anything to do with the client at the Bloomsbury apartment? The one you mysteriously bailed on?'

'Oh, Kitty, it has everything to do with Stefanos,' Claudia said. 'He's a man from my past. Do you remember me telling you about my first love? The guy in Santorini?'

'*Him*? The billionaire that got away?'

'The very one. Stefanos Adrastos.'

Kitty's eyes widened. 'I can't believe it. Did he plan it? Or was it an amazing coincidence?

Come and sit down. I'll pour you some wine and you can tell me all about it.'

Kitty led her to Sebastian's grandmother's private sitting room, which Kitty had appropriated for her own, and sat her down on the sofa next to her. No sooner had she poured Claudia some wine than she pounced on her for details of why she'd so suddenly left the packing job—something she'd never done before.

Her friend was enthralled by Claudia's story of her first, long-lost love showing up in London as a client of PWP, and what had happened after she'd gone to his hotel for coffee.

'Break-up sex postponed for ten years?' Kitty said. 'That's powerful stuff.'

Kitty had nailed it, Claudia thought. Of course that was all it had been. Really good sex between people who hadn't forgotten how to please each other in bed. They certainly hadn't made any promises to each other—not even a nominal stab at being friends. And yet it had been so perfect. *He* had been so perfect.

'Stefanos is indeed very powerful,' Claudia said with a laugh. 'And he is *so* sexy.'

'So what are you doing here with me?' Kitty asked. 'Why aren't you with him right now? Are you going to see him again?'

Claudia sipped her wine. 'We did talk about seeing each other again next time he's in London. But I'm not sure it will happen again—going to bed with him, I mean.'

'Do you want it to happen again?'

'In terms of sheer physical pleasure, yes. But it's complicated. And I mean *really* complicated. He's been married and divorced twice.'

'Perhaps he never really got over you?'

'I suspect he could still be bitter. Remember I refused his proposal and left him.'

'So he's bitter and twisted?'

'Not twisted—perhaps bitter. Heaven knows what caused his divorces. He wouldn't tell me. That said, he's every bit as gorgeous as he was ten years ago.' She knew she wasn't keeping the longing from her voice. 'Even more handsome, and super self-assured and confident.'

'Seems he finds you gorgeous too.'

'There is that… But you know I've never been one for casual hook-ups.'

'You haven't actually dated anyone since you got back to the UK.'

Claudia had met Kitty at a public relations function at a hotel years ago, when Kitty had been a baby PR person and Claudia in her first job. They'd stayed friends during all the years Claudia had been out of the country.

'PWP takes up all my time and energy,' Claudia said, aware of the defensive note to her voice.

She knew that wasn't quite true. The episode in Sydney with Brad had made her deeply distrustful—too distrustful to consider using dating apps—and she hadn't met anyone who interested her at a bar or a party or any other likely places. She'd been too distrustful, in fact, to spend time with any man. Until Stefanos had opened the door of that apartment in Bloomsbury and there he'd stood. The only man she had ever truly loved.

'I think you could find the time and certainly the energy if the person was right,' said Kitty carefully.

Claudia picked up her glass. 'That's it… I can't help feeling that Stefanos is the right person—always was the right person. But I lost my chance with him ten years ago. And that chance won't come again. Stefanos even has a saying about it in Greek: you can't step in the same river twice.'

'That sounds grim. And very definite.'

'Even if I wanted to see him, the ball is very firmly in his court. We both hurt each other in the past, and I'm not sure he would want to tear old scars open again. I'd be wary too.'

'It's a real case of *what if?*, isn't it?' said Kitty.

'It is.' Claudia took a sip from her wine and put the glass back on the coffee table. 'What if I'd stayed with Stefanos in Greece when I was nineteen? Dropped out of uni and never gone home?'

'You would have grown to resent him,' Kitty said firmly.

'Would I?'

'Yes. You would have always been asking yourself what if you'd followed your dream career instead of being a teenage bride.'

'What if I'd *liked* being a teenage bride? Plenty of girls do.'

Simply being with Stefanos might have been enough.

'Maybe you would have—who knows?' said Kitty. 'Maybe you'd have had four children by now.'

'I don't think so.'

She thought about how much Stefanos had wanted a baby back then. Would he have wanted four kids? It seemed odd that he was now thirty and didn't have children.

'You would certainly have had enough money never to worry about how many kids you had,' Kitty said.

'It was never about his money with Stefanos and me. I thought he was just a guy working on some rich person's yacht for the summer when I first met him. I would have felt the same about him if that had been the truth.'

'It has never been an issue with me and Sebastian either.'

Sebastian was a self-made millionaire, but had

also inherited billions. He'd been Kitty's boss before he had been her husband.

'Turned out Stefanos *was* the rich person who owned the yacht. I wonder if he still has it? We never got around to talking about stuff like that.'

'Too busy getting down and dirty in his hotel room?' Kitty teased.

'It wasn't dirty! Well, maybe just a little…and decidedly delicious,' Claudia said, with a small smile of remembered pleasure.

It had been so delicious she wanted to close her eyes and relive those moments. It was good to talk with Kitty about it. She certainly couldn't talk to anyone else.

'You'll never know if you made the right or wrong decision back then. It's that "sliding doors" thing, isn't it?' Kitty said. 'But, as your friend, I'd say you did make the right decision. You've had a good career doing what you loved, you've seen the world, and now you have a successful business. If you hadn't made that decision back then in Santorini we wouldn't be friends, and I'd be sad about that.'

'Only you wouldn't know I existed, so how could you be sad?'

Kitty laughed. 'True.'

Claudia paused. 'One part of me wants to hop on a plane and land at his door in Athens, ask if there could be a second chance for us. We were so good before—could we not be good again? We're older, I've got travel out of my system.'

'And the other part of you?'

Claudia sighed. 'The other part knows I wouldn't dare. Today was perfect. I should leave it as it is. We talked about stuff we should have talked about ten years ago. Perhaps he doesn't feel so bitter towards me now. And we had the break-up sex we didn't have back then.'

'Which has left you wanting more,' said Kitty.

'But what if it was so good *because* it was so unexpected and *because* it brought closure of a kind? It mightn't be like that again.' Although it had always been good with Stefanos, even after a ten-year break. 'The truth of it is, I don't know if I can trust him. Is he really single? He might be twice divorced and never want to get married again, but that doesn't stop him having a girlfriend. Imagine if she opened the door to me when I went knocking? He broke my heart ten years ago. I don't want to risk getting my heart broken again. It's best to leave things as they are. Looking back, I can see it took me years to get over him.'

'Did you ever really get over him?' Kitty asked gently.

'Of course I did.'

Kitty raised her eyebrows. 'If you say so.'

'He did say he'd be back in London and we'd

meet for lunch. That is if he doesn't ghost me again.'

'Do you really think he'd do that?'

'Who knows what he might do?'

CHAPTER EIGHT

To Claudia's utter relief, Stefanos didn't ghost her after their unexpected reunion. In fact he texted her almost as soon as he'd returned to Athens. She'd picked up her phone with unsteady hands, heart pumping, mouth dry. Only to be plunged into the depths of disappointment when she'd read his words, saying how nice it had been to meet her in such an unexpected way.

A few friendly yet equally impersonal texts had followed. So that was all it would be. She'd given up checking her messages with any degree of anticipation. Yes, it was a little hurtful that he didn't appear to have seen anything memorable and remarkable in the morning they'd spent together in bed. But he'd made no promises of anything more—and neither, in fact, had she, as she had to remind herself.

On the other hand, she found her memories of that day became more special: the incredible coincidence of their reunion, their glorious lovemaking. It wasn't going to happen again, but she hoped there would be a chance to catch up with him. There was so much more she wanted to know about what had happened to him in the ten years between their meetings. She would have to be content with that.

Claudia threw herself into her work like never before—taking extra bookings, doing extra marketing calls. She doubled her sessions at the gym and binge-watched too much television in the evenings. Anything to take her mind off Stefanos. Not that she thought of him all the time. But he popped up in her thoughts more often than she liked, and it was disconcerting.

Six weeks after he'd gone back to Athens, she began to wonder if she was overdoing it. She was more fatigued than she could ever remember being. She was too tired to eat much, and when she did she felt nauseous. In fact the nausea and fatigue increased so much she cut back on her long hours and the exercise. But she still didn't feel well—although the nausea came and went.

It was so frustrating when she was used to enjoying perfect health and energy around the clock. A virus? She must have succumbed to a virus. But a test proved negative. Some kind of food allergy? But she hadn't changed her diet.

A few weeks later, when she had time she went for an appointment with her GP.

'Have you done a pregnancy test?' the doctor asked, as soon as Claudia had recited her symptoms.

Claudia stared at her. 'I'm not pregnant,' she said immediately.

She couldn't possibly be pregnant.

And yet when the doctor asked the date of her last period it seemed she might have missed one. But a lot of exercise and stress could cause that, couldn't it?

'It's a good idea to rule pregnancy out,' the doctor said.

She handed Claudia a pregnancy test and told her where the bathroom was.

Pregnant? From one morning with Stefanos? One morning when they'd been careful with contraception? She simply couldn't be.

Panic seized her, making her feel shaky and anxious. She nearly dropped the test stick into the loo.

Get a grip, Claudia, she told herself. *The doctor said the test is to rule pregnancy out.*

It was a very long three minutes while she waited for the result.

But it didn't rule it out.

The test showed a resounding positive result. Two blue lines said she was pregnant.

She stared at it for a long time, willing the result to go away. The last thing she'd expected to be at this stage of her life was unmarried and pregnant.

'How accurate is this test?' she asked the doctor, once again sitting across the desk from her in her consulting room.

'Very accurate,' the doctor said. 'Are you okay with being pregnant, Claudia?'

'I… I'll have to get used to the idea,' she said. 'It wasn't planned.'

Had she been in denial about what the nausea and fatigue had meant? Kidded herself that it was the push-ups at the gym that had made her breasts a size larger? Or had she simply not recognised the implications.

'I'll need to examine you,' the doctor said.

Claudia lay on the examination table, her thoughts racing. *Pregnant.* How was she going to manage this? Stefanos! Would she tell him? *Should* she tell him? Did he have a right to know? What would he think? What did it mean for PWP?

'You're definitely pregnant,' the doctor said. 'I'd estimate about eight weeks along.'

'I can tell you the exact day I conceived,' Claudia said.

'You can be that sure?'

'Absolutely. It was the only time I'd had sex in a long time.'

'And the father?'

'Not around,' she said. 'We're not in a relationship and he lives in another country. I'm in this on my own.'

'Do you want to keep the baby?' the doctor said.

Claudia was surprised at the sudden burst of possessiveness she felt towards her baby. She put her hand on her stomach. *Her baby.* How quickly she'd come to think that way.

'Absolutely I'm keeping this baby,' she said. She even managed a laugh. 'You know, I've never seen myself as a mother. But suddenly I know that I really want this baby.' She paused. 'It feels right.'

Excitement began to stir. Her life was about to change irrevocably.

The doctor smiled. 'That's wonderful.'

Claudia felt dazed. This had happened so quickly. 'It *is* wonderful, isn't it?'

'There's a lot of help available for sole parents—including financial help,' the doctor said.

'I'll be okay,' Claudia said. 'I have my own business. I can manage.'

'Do you know much about the father?'

'He…he's actually an old acquaintance. But as I said it was a…a one-off thing.'

'The reason I ask is that there will be screening tests available throughout your pregnancy that, among other things, look for the possibility of inherited conditions. It's helpful if the father takes part in some of those tests.'

'To be honest, I don't know if he will want to be involved, and if so to what extent.'

'One thing you might ask him is what his blood type is. You are Rh-negative. If you conceive an Rh-positive baby, there can be consequences. Have you had any previous pregnancies or miscarriages?'

'No,' Claudia said. 'I thought I was pregnant once, but it was a false alarm.'

'A false alarm can be an early miscarriage. It would be a good thing to find out the father's blood group if you can. It's important.'

Now she had no choice. She would have to tell Stefanos she was pregnant and she dreaded it.

She stumbled out of the doctor's surgery, clutching a handful of pregnancy information leaflets, unable to think of anything else but what Stefanos's reaction might be. In doing so, she passed a mother wheeling a pram with a young baby in it. She couldn't help but look, and was swept by a surge of unexpected emotion at the sight of its sweet little face and the unblinking eyes looking up at her.

She was not the kind of woman who gushed over strange babies in prams. Until now.

'Your baby is beautiful,' she said, unable to take her eyes off the baby. Those tiny starfish hands. That fine, wispy hair. The little rosebud mouth. The sheer adorableness of this little one.

'He is, isn't he? Thank you,' the mother said, smiling, looking lovingly into the pram. She looked at the leaflets. 'Are you expecting?'

'Yes—yes, I am,' Claudia said. 'Due some time in January.'

'Congratulations,' the other woman said. She looked fondly down at her baby. 'Best thing I ever did was to have this little man.'

Claudia was swept by a sudden wave of joy and she couldn't stop smiling.

She was going to be a mother. And she couldn't be happier about it.

Claudia sat on her news for the next two days. She simply couldn't find the strength to get in touch with Stefanos. He had sent her a text to say he had plans to visit London soon, and hoped they'd be able to catch up, but had given no definite date. She hadn't yet replied.

She couldn't ask him about his blood group by text. It would have to be a phone call—and that terrified her. She was not the procrastinating type, and yet she kept putting the call off. But the doctor had stressed how important it was to get the father's information.

She knew she'd delayed as long as she could. She sat down in the living room, took a deep breath, and picked up her phone. She would start by chatting about his forthcoming visit, and then ease into a query about his blood group.

Athens was two hours ahead of London. It was just before lunch his time. With thumbs that seemed suddenly clumsy, she keyed in his number.

She'd startled him—that was obvious when he answered—and she wondered if there had been a moment when he had thought about not answering…when he'd seen the caller ID on his phone had shown *Claudia Eaton*. Calling him out of the blue hadn't really been part of their deal.

'Is this a good time?' she asked tentatively.

'An excellent time. I'm at home.'

At the sound of his voice, so deep and manly, still with that charming trace of accent when he spoke in English, she felt her prepared speech fly out of her mind. Instead, she dived in headlong.

'Er… I… I need to ask you about your blood group. I don't have a clue what it is. Of all the things we talked about, we never talked about that. Well…well, why would we?'

This was so difficult.

'My blood group?'

She could hear the puzzled frown in his voice. She hadn't meant to hit him with it like that.

'Why would you want to know that?'

'Tell me and I'll tell you.'

That had not been the right thing to say—she knew it as soon as the words escaped her lips. It would make him suspicious. She wanted to disconnect the call and pretend it never happened.

'No one has ever asked me that before,' he said, and indeed his voice was underscored with suspicion.

Would he put two and two together? She'd been surprised at how little any of the few people she'd told about her pregnancy knew about potential rhesus factor complications.'

'Please just tell me,' she said.

Had he picked up the anxiety in her voice? Because now he answered immediately.

'O negative.'

'Oh,' she said.

'Why, *"oh"*?'

'Relief. That's good news.' No matter how she said it, this was not going to be easy. 'I… I'm Rh negative and…and…' her words spilled out in a rush '…it turns out I'm pregnant and it could be a problem if the father is Rh positive. But he isn't—he's negative. That is…*you're* negative.'

At his end there was silence for a moment. Then, 'You're pregnant? By me?'

She nodded, then realised he couldn't see her. 'Yes. There's no doubt. There…there wasn't anyone for a long time before you and…and there hasn't been anyone since.'

Another silence told her that if some part of her had hoped he would be pleased at the news that wasn't the case. She felt sick. Not sick with the morning sickness that she hadn't recognised as an early sign of her pregnancy, but sick with trepidation at his reaction.

'This is…a shock,' he said. 'We were careful.'

'Not careful enough, it seems.' She paused, but he didn't fill the silence. 'I'm not asking anything of you, Stefanos,' she said. 'Please be reassured of that. But I needed to know your blood group. This might be a second pregnancy for me with you as the father. I might have had a miscarriage before. It can be dangerous if the baby is found to be Rh positive, inherited from the father.'

'A second pregnancy? But—'

'My doctor said a ten-days-late period can be a very early miscarriage.' This was so difficult to explain on the phone, where she couldn't read his face. 'If it was an actual pregnancy back then, my body might have set up antibodies against an Rh positive baby—which could harm it. That's why I had to ask you. But if you're negative, and I'm negative, no dangerous sensitivity can develop and we're okay. Well, the baby is okay. Thankfully.'

Another pause. Then, 'When were you going to tell me you're pregnant?'

Claudia didn't know the answer to that herself. 'I... I don't know. It's early days yet. I didn't want a repeat of last time.'

How could she possibly have called him, told him she was pregnant, and then found out she was just late and history had repeated itself when her period came? She'd had to be certain. If she hadn't had to ask him about his blood group she would have waited until twelve weeks, which people said was a safer time to let people know.

'You're definitely pregnant?'

'There's no doubt. The doctor has confirmed it. Eight weeks.'

There was silence. Was he counting back the days to their time in that hotel in Bloomsbury?

'What do you feel about the pregnancy?' he asked.

Was he asking her, in a roundabout way, whether she intended to continue with the pregnancy? She couldn't blame him. She had made it clear, even at their recent meeting, that marriage and children weren't on her life plan.

'Shock. Disbelief. Acceptance. And finally... joy. Yes, joy. It might surprise you, considering what I've said to you before, but I... I want this baby very much. I'm not nineteen this time. The prospect of a baby from the perspective of being twenty-nine with my own business, is very different from the prospect as a nineteen-year-old student.'

'That's quite a turnaround,' he said.

He was choosing his words carefully, she thought.

'Back then…as we've both said…it was a different world. *I'm* different now. At a different stage of life.'

'What role do you expect me to play?'

No instant proposal of marriage this time.

'Whatever we sort out. Between us. You can have as much access as you want.'

She had adored her father, and would do all she could to make sure Stefanos played a role in their child's life.

Another pause. Then, 'I need to think about this,' he said. 'It's quite a shock.'

Her voice caught. 'It was for me too.'

'Are you all right? Health-wise, I mean?'

'Feeling a little fragile, to be honest. But it's early days yet. I'm taking it easy…having some time off work and not packing boxes or doing heavy work. The doctor said it will get better.'

Claudia hoped she was right. She'd been prepared for morning sickness, but recently it had intensified—morning, noon and night sickness had come as quite a shock.

'Make sure you look after yourself,' Stefanos said.

His words sounded so impersonal—but what had she expected? She'd made such a big deal of telling him how independent she was, and how she didn't need a man in her life. Only just a few kind words would make a difference. She hadn't realised how vulnerable being pregnant would make her feel.

'I will,' she said. 'I'll put my feet up and read through the pile of "what to expect" books I've had delivered. And I need to call the doctor's surgery to tell them about your blood group.' She paused. 'Thank you, Stefanos.'

Why had she felt the need to thank him? For not being Rh positive? For being an involuntary sperm donor? For not berating her for getting pregnant in an effort to trap herself a billionaire?

She knew he wouldn't believe that of her.

Or would he?

Stefanos put down his phone on the table where he sat near the swimming pool at his Athens mansion—his favourite spot to have lunch, overlooking the harbour. For a long time he simply stared into the aqua blue waters of the pool, sparkling in the sunshine.

Claudia was pregnant with his baby. He didn't doubt the truth of that. What he wasn't sure was how he felt about it. His two divorces had done a lot to kill his long-held desire to have children. If you had a child with a woman you were tied to her, whether you wanted to be or not. He shuddered at the thought of being tied to a person like Tiana for life.

If he didn't have such a painful history with Claudia…if he didn't have those two disastrous marriages behind him…he would ask Claudia to marry him. It would be expected of him. It would be the right thing to do. He was still attracted to her—there was no doubt about that. *Man, was he still attracted to her…* But he didn't actually know her any more.

She'd done a good job of hiding her family history and her motivations back in Santorini. Who was to say there weren't other secrets she was hiding? And he still wasn't sure if theirs had been a relationship based only on sex, and that wouldn't weather everyday life together.

And yet there was a child on the way—*his* child.

The news was something that years ago he would have rejoiced at and celebrated with vintage champagne. But that had been then. Now he had become so mired in distrust he'd given up on the idea of a family. But the more he thought about Claudia being pregnant, the more those long-buried feelings about holding his child in his arms and a future with his son or daughter, infiltrated the barriers he had erected around his emotions.

Yes, he wanted a child very much. But he did not want any attachment to its mother.

No way would he let himself be trapped in a loveless marriage for a third time—baby or no baby. He'd made grave misjudgements about the women he'd married—especially with Tiana. He was not going to tread that path again.

Tiana had pretended to be something she was not. It had only been after he'd married her that he'd discovered she was older than she'd claimed to be, and already had a child with another man. She had never stopped taking the contraceptive pill.

What kind of woman hid her child from the man she'd married because she'd had an eye on that man's money? And what kind of blindly trusting man didn't pick up on the discrepancies in her story? That man no longer existed. He would never take a woman at face value again. If a woman like Tiana had called out of the blue to tell him she was pregnant his first call would be to his lawyer.

But deep in his gut Stefanos knew Claudia wasn't like Tiana. A person surely didn't change her intrinsic nature that much even after ten years.

For one thing, she had never displayed the slightest sign of greed when it came to his considerable fortune. Back in Bloomsbury she had insisted on paying her share for the coffee in the hotel and their room service lunch. That had come as quite a novelty to him. Even his friends expected him to pick up the tab—it came with the billionaire turf.

But he'd been shocked by her revelations about her family and the reasons why she'd been so anti-marriage—something so important and yet she'd withheld that from him.

Still, he was worried about her. She'd obviously been making an effort to sound chipper, but he'd heard the weariness underlying her voice.

She was pregnant with his child.

She did a strenuous, physical job.

She might have miscarried before. Wouldn't that make her vulnerable to miscarriage again?

Now he had accepted the idea of this baby, he discovered he didn't want to lose it.

His mother had suffered miscarriage after miscarriage, both before and after having him. It had been the heartbreak of his parents' lives. Somehow he'd thought he had to make it up to them, as the only child upon whom all their hopes and expectations were centred. That was why he'd agreed to put aside his interest in history and archaeology to go into the family business—even though it wasn't what he'd have chosen. And that was why he'd known from a young age that he wanted a family of his own—why he'd offered to marry Claudia back then.

He wanted this baby with a fierce yearning. A baby was a gift. He didn't have to marry Claudia—that was assuming she'd even entertained thoughts of marrying him. But he had to look after her. And their child. The sooner the better.

CHAPTER NINE

THE NEXT MORNING, busy brushing her teeth in the bathroom of her maisonette in Hammersmith, Claudia didn't at first hear the repeated buzzing of the doorbell downstairs. The maisonette, in a converted period house, comprised a small entry hall on ground level, with a coat rack—and maybe enough room for a pram—and a set of narrow stairs leading up to a reception room, the kitchen, the bathroom and two bedrooms—the smaller one used as her home office.

'Urgh…' she muttered to herself as she brushed her teeth—again—and washed out her mouth. This morning sickness was really getting out of hand.

'Don't fight the nausea in the morning, give in to it,' her mother had advised. 'Then try a dry cracker when your tummy settles.'

That was all very well—until the next bout of nausea hit.

She kept checking the books, reading about

the developmental stages of the baby, worrying that he or she wasn't getting enough nourishment because 'the mother'—*her*...she was still getting used to that idea!—wasn't keeping enough food down.

Claudia secured her long kimono-style wrap around her waist and headed to the door. She wasn't expecting a parcel. It was too early to start buying baby things, and she didn't want to jinx the pregnancy until she was past twelve weeks and had had her first dating scan. But what else could it be?

She looked through the intercom camera. A tall, broad-shouldered man filled the steps outside. *Not the postman.* She felt what little colour she'd had left in her face drain away. She opened the door with a shaky hand.

'Stefanos. What are you doing here?'

'I've come to see how you are. You didn't sound well when we spoke yesterday.'

'But how...?'

'Very early flight,' he said.

Did Stefanos get even more handsome each time she saw him? His hair was slightly longer, his beard shorter, and he was wearing charcoal trousers, a white linen shirt with the sleeves rolled up to show tanned forearms, and black sneakers with thick white soles. He looked as if he'd stepped off the page of a glossy men's fashion magazine. He wore dark sunglasses, but took them off as he spoke.

'*Kalimera,*' he said cheerfully—*good morning* in Greek.

'Uh…*kalimera*,' Claudia mumbled.

She was suddenly aware of how dishevelled she must seem to him—hair a mess, no make-up, still not dressed. She prided herself on looking well groomed. She even ironed her leggings and T-shirts for work and polished her trainers. But she simply didn't have the energy to care about how she looked now.

She clutched the neckline of her silky wrap—at least it was clean—to close it tighter. 'Come in. The living room is up the stairs.'

The tiny entrance hall seemed suddenly filled with tall, powerful Greek male. She almost danced around him to avoid contact. He gestured to her to go first up the stairs. She was utterly aware of him—his height, his strength, his scent. Even in her weakened state, he still made her shaky at the knees.

'Nice apartment,' Stefanos said, looking around him as he got to the top of the stairs.

The room was light and airy, with windows that faced south. The landlord had painted the apartment an off-white before she'd moved in, and the bathroom and kitchen were fairly new. She'd kept the furnishings neutral, with cushions and throws in beautiful Batik fabrics from Bali, and other souvenirs of her travels. With a baby on the way, she'd have to shelve plans to buy her own place. She would need all her savings.

'I like it, and the rent is reasonable for this area,' she said.

Why did she feel she had to explain?

He frowned. 'You don't own your place?'

'I'm working on it,' she said. *Welcome to the world of everyday folk*, she thought, but didn't dare say. Her entire maisonette would fit into the living room of his Bloomsbury apartment with room to spare.

'Can I get you a coffee?' she asked without thinking, simply from force of habit when a guest arrived.

'Yes, I—'

But just the mention of coffee, the thought of the smell of coffee, had made the nausea rise again.

'Excuse me, I—'

That was all she could manage before she made a dash to the bathroom and slammed the door behind her. More retching, more teeth-brushing, more splashing of cold water on her face.

Why did Stefanos have to visit right now?

She emerged to find Stefanos looking out of the window, which looked over to the small garden below that she shared with the other two maisonettes in the building.

He spun around to face her. 'You look terrible,' he said bluntly.

She managed a watery smile. 'I guess I do. Nice of you to say so.'

'I didn't mean to insult you. I was speaking the truth. You're obviously not well.'

'Morning sickness is a normal part of pregnancy,' she said.

'But to be this ill? You look like you've lost weight, not gained it.'

'It is worse than I thought it would be,' she admitted. 'But the doctor says the sickness will pass.' So did all the pregnancy books she'd read.

'How are you managing with your job?' he asked.

'I'm not,' she said. 'I don't want to take any chances with lifting and heavy work. I'm just doing admin at home. We've been training a very good woman to take over most of Kitty's duties. She's able to step in for me too.'

Even the paperwork was an effort with her constant nausea and tiredness. She wasn't sleeping well. Truth was, she felt dreadful—but she didn't want to admit it to him.

'What about eating?'

She knew her smile was on the wan side.

'That's not such an issue as I'm too nauseous to eat much.'

He strode back and forth the length of her living room. 'Is anyone helping you?'

'I don't need help. I can manage on my own—plenty of women do. And my mum is on the phone any time I need her. She's ecstatic at the prospect of being a grandma. She's never actually seen the Australian grandchildren. And the twins are looking forward to being aunties.'

'That's all very well, but how long since you've actually had a vacation?'

'I went to my family in Swindon for Christmas.'

He frowned. 'I mean a proper break?'

She thought about it. 'Not since we started the business, nearly three years ago. There's been no time for holidays for either Kitty or me. Besides, the recent world situation has made it difficult to travel.'

Stefanos made an exclamation of dismay. 'You obviously need rest and proper nourishment. For both your sake and…and the baby's.'

It was the first time he'd mentioned the baby.

'Kitty sends me yummy care packages whipped up by her cook.' She couldn't tell Kitty that the gourmet food usually didn't stay down. 'I do my best,' she said.

'But is it enough?'

'I'm sure I can manage. I was very healthy before I got pregnant.' She paused. 'That… I mean me getting pregnant… I… I was as shocked as you. I thought I had food poisoning, or an allergy. I can assure you that you are the father, but I won't be offended if…if you want a DNA test. Apparently a test can be done with no risk of harm to the baby while I'm pregnant, or it can be done after the baby is born.'

For some reason just talking about it made her feel tearful. She'd been up-and-down emotional for weeks—apparently due to the fluctuating hormones of pregnancy. But having to explain to people that the baby's father was out of the picture, that she didn't know his blood group, and that she intended to be a lone parent was stressful. Asking about DNA tests at a local centre had been embarrassing. She was sure the receptionist had automatically assumed she was uncertain who the father was and needed to clarify which of a number of men it could be. Although Claudia would rather they believed that than know that the billionaire father of her baby would want a DNA test in case she was a gold-digger making a false claim to his fortune.

'I don't need a DNA test,' Stefanos said.

'But I—'

'I don't believe you would lie about something so important.'

She looked up at him, unable to stop her eyes from misting with tears. 'Thank you, Stefanos, that means a lot. I… I…can't tell you how much it means.' Frantically she scrubbed at her eyes with her fists. 'I'm not crying. I'm really not. It's just that I feel so unwell, and I'm so tired, and I'm overwhelmed, and…and I'm terrified.'

Despite her every effort to suppress them, she burst into full-on sobs.

Stefanos immediately drew her into a hug. He had broad, accommodating shoulders and he wrapped his arms around her and let her cry.

Finally, she sobbed herself out. Her breathing evened out except for the odd gulp and the occasional sniffle. She stilled, wishing she could stay there for ever and not have to face him after making such an exhibition of herself.

That had been one of her grandmother's expressions when Claudia had lost her temper or started to cry—or, as a teenager, had had too much to drink. Grandma Eaton had had quite a lot to do with her and Mark's upbringing while her parents had been busy at the pub. And apparently Claudia, as a child, had quite often made 'an exhibition of herself' and had to be reprimanded. No wonder she'd grown up tamping down on strong emotions, determined to present the best possible view of herself to others.

Finally, she reluctantly pulled away from Stefanos, feeling as if she was leaving a safe haven. She looked up at him and was relieved to see kindness, not criticism, in his eyes.

'I'm sorry. I didn't mean—' she started.

'Do you remember what I said about not saying sorry? You have absolutely nothing to be sorry about.' He wiped a damp strand of hair away from her face in a gesture that was surprisingly tender.

'Your shirt! Oh, no, there are wet patches.' Ineffectually, she tried to dab them away with the sleeve of her wrap. 'Luckily I wasn't wearing make-up, so no mascara stains at least.'

'Just salty tears,' he said, sounding more than a touch amused. 'They'll dry.'

'But…but that nice linen fabric could be rumpled. Let me iron your shirt—it's the least I can do.'

'There is absolutely no need for you to do that, Claudia.'

'If you're sure…but it's no trouble. And—'

'What I want you to do is tell me why you're so terrified of having a baby.'

Stefanos led Claudia to her sofa—a fragile Claudia who didn't look pregnant except for the notable swelling of her breasts. She seemed thinner than when he had last held her in his arms. That couldn't be right if she was eight weeks along.

'Come and sit down,' he said. 'Can I get you a drink?'

'That…that would be nice. There's some fizzy mineral water in the fridge. I… I seem to be able to keep that down.'

He headed towards the refrigerator in her compact kitchen.

'Help yourself to any drink you like,' she said. 'Although I… I'd ask you not to make coffee. Even the smell of it makes me nauseous.'

He carried two glasses of chilled mineral water to the coffee table near the sofa. 'Nothing to eat?'

'Please, no,' she said, wiping her hand across her forehead. Her eyes were reddened and her hair straggled across her face. It made her seem vulnerable, and yet somehow did not detract from how attractive he found her.

She slowly took a few sips of cold water, closed her eyes, and sat back in the sofa.

'Better?' he asked. He angled himself so that, while he stayed at a distance, he could still clearly see her face.

She nodded. 'Thank you.'

'So tell me why you're terrified.'

She sniffed. 'Can I start with why I'm feeling overwhelmed?'

'It's a good enough place to start.'

'First of all—as you know—I had no plans

for starting a family. Not within marriage, and certainly not outside it.'

He started to say something, but she put up her hand in a halt sign.

'Not that there is anything wrong with having a baby when you're not married. Lots of women do it and are wonderful mothers. As I will be, of course.'

His very conservative family would definitely think it was a problem. A major problem. But he had no intention of telling his mother anything about Claudia. He loved his *mitera*, but he still hadn't quite forgiven her for encouraging his marriage to Arina when she'd known full well that Arina's mother had suspected her daughter was gay. And he would not be forced into marriage with the mother of his child simply because not marrying her would be socially unacceptable.

'Of course,' he said.

'But a baby is a lot of work—as I know only too well. How I'll manage motherhood and running my own business is concerning me. Again, lots of women do it, and I'm sure I'll manage, but everything I'll have to put in place is a tad overwhelming.'

Stefanos didn't want to offer help at this stage. Not until he'd really got his mind around the fact that he was going to be a father but not under the circumstances he'd dreamed of. He would definitely offer financial help. Lifelong support for his child was a given. And who knew? If Claudia decided she really couldn't manage a baby he would ask for custody and she could have visitation rights, rather than the other way around. But, again, it was too soon to bring that up. He didn't know how she would take it.

It was less than twenty-four hours since Claudia had dropped the baby bombshell on him. He needed to speak to a lawyer before he committed to anything. He'd learned that lesson from his dealings with Tiana.

'And the terror?' he asked.

'Does it sound cowardly to admit that I'm actually scared of childbirth? One of the ladies who packs for us had a baby last year and she said it was literally like passing a watermelon. The birth videos I've watched online are nothing short of horrific. Do you ever watch that television show about midwives?'

'Er…no. Why would I?' He couldn't imagine anything worse.

'Don't.' She shuddered. 'It's quite scary. Admittedly, it's all lovely at the end, with the mums having forgotten the ordeal they've been through once they have their babies in their arms.'

'But can it be that bad if so many women have babies? More than one baby?'

'Rationally, yes, you'd think not. The human race continues to thrive. But my fear is irrational. Maybe because my mother had such a difficult time with the twins. And…er… I shouldn't admit to it, but I'm not sure I like the idea of breastfeeding—even if it's the best thing for the baby.' She paused to take a deep breath. 'There's another thing I worry about. Mum told me she had bad morning sickness because she was having twins. What if *I'm* having twins? The doctor says there's a chance, if a small one.' She took another cautious sip of water. 'Remember I told you what it was like for my family?'

He knew he'd have to tread carefully here. 'It would be different if you were their mother.'

'It would still be as much work, and with no sixteen-year-old daughter to help me like my mum had. Would I be able to cope?'

Stefanos had to stop himself from saying that of course he would pay for a nanny. Two nannies if she needed them. As many nannies as she wanted. The time wasn't right for that yet.

'I understand your fears, but surely in London there are good doctors and midwives to help you?'

'Of course there are. I'm probably worrying too much. I've only been on leave since Monday—yesterday, that is. Two days into the week and I've probably already spent too much time on my own, worrying and…and brooding.'

An idea that had been formulating in his mind since he'd first seen her downstairs and been shocked at how frail she looked suddenly crystallised. 'I have the answer to some of your problems. You need a holiday and you need to be looked after. I have a villa on the privately owned Greek island of Kosmimo.'

Her eyes widened. 'Kosmimo? That fabulous resort Pevezzo Athina—isn't that on Kosmimo?'

He nodded. 'It most certainly is. It's owned by my cousin Alex and his wife Dell.'

'Wait…that's meant to be the most amazing resort. One of the most acclaimed in Europe. I've dreamed of visiting it. That is…'

'If you could ever bring yourself to visit Greece again?'

'Yes.'

'Can you overcome your reluctance to go to Greece and stay with me on Kosmimo?'

'I… I don't know what to say.'

'Just say yes. It could be just what you need. Pevezzo Athina is a very upscale health resort, as well as a six-star hotel. Good food, relaxation… medical help not far away if you need it.'

She couldn't meet his gaze. 'Go with you? As…as what?'

'I could say you can pretend to be my fiancée,

but I won't. There has been too much deception in my life. If you agree, we'll say you're a former girlfriend, that we met again by chance recently, renewed our friendship and…and perhaps weren't as careful about contraception as we should have been.'

'I don't know that we'll need to go into that much detail. We *were* careful. No contraception is one hundred percent effective—but heaven knows what went wrong that morning.'

He could only remember what had gone absolutely *right* that morning. Sex with beautiful, sensuous Claudia. Memories of her had rarely been out of his mind since. But he was still not sure about letting his former lover back into his life. Her pregnancy had brought them together in a way he had never envisaged.

'Agreed. But Dell has a way of getting confidences out of people, so be warned.'

'So, quite simply, what you're saying is that we tell the truth.'

What a relief it was for him to hear her say that. *The truth.* 'Yes.'

'And about…about the accommodation…?'

'I have a villa on the island, which is used by guests when I'm not in residence. It's very private, with its own swimming pool. But you can also use the facilities of the hotel. It's a beautiful island. I think you'll like it.'

Again, she couldn't meet his gaze. 'And the…
er…bedroom situation?'

'Two separate suites. You in one—me in the
other.'

'What about the airfare?'

'There is no need for you to worry about air-
fares or any other expense.'

'But I can't allow that. I—'

'You are giving me a child, Claudia. Please
allow me to look after you.'

She paused for a long moment, and he could
see her debating her independence against her
need for help. Then, 'Thank you. I have to say it
sounds absolutely wonderful. When do we go?'

'Right now—as soon as you can pack your
bags.'

CHAPTER TEN

IF STEFANOS HADN'T caught her when she'd been feeling at such an impossibly low ebb, no way would Claudia have agreed to let him whisk her away to a luxury resort where she wouldn't know a soul. But he'd caught her at a super-vulnerable moment and had been unexpectedly kind, rather than acting the domineering Greek male.

No wonder she'd gone to mush. It had made absolute sense to go with him. Even though she knew she needed to confront him about what he'd meant by his words, *'You're giving me a child.'*

Because she most definitely was *not* giving him her child. She was offering to share her child with him, for the child's sake.

The huge discrepancy between her wealth and power and his was beginning to scare her into thinking he might intend to make a claim on the baby. In some ways she regretted telling him she had never wanted to get married or have a family. Or opened up on her worries about childbirth and how she was going to manage being both sole parent and a businesswoman. Could he use that information against her if a custody battle eventuated?

She knew she would have to talk with him about their expectations concerning the baby they had conceived that unexpected and exciting day in Bloomsbury eight weeks ago. But she would have to stay wary and pick her moment.

And now, a few hours later, with the large backpack that had seen her through her travels hastily packed with summer clothes, she was boarding a private jet with him. The 'very early flight' he'd caught to Heathrow had clearly been waiting for his return and they were heading to Athens.

She had never flown in a private plane before, although she tried to act cool, as if it wasn't something out of her experience. The jet was just like in the movies—all leather seats and luxury and a very attentive crew. She was glad she'd dressed in grape-coloured narrow linen trousers, a stylish cream silk knit top and a light linen jacket, so she didn't look out of place. Her right wrist jangled with the copper bangles she'd been told staved off morning sickness, but they didn't seem to be having any effect.

It was a shame she was unable to eat anything

for fear of feeling nauseous, because the food on offer looked delicious.

The flight was smooth and trouble-free and she slept for most of it. Stefanos told her a little about his cousin Alex and his wife Dell. Alex was Greek-Australian, born in Sydney, and Claudia soon realised she knew of him.

Alex Mikhalis was considered a legend on the Sydney hospitality scene. He was a nightclub and restaurant mogul whose fiancée had been killed in a hostage situation at one of his restaurants. A broken man, he'd returned to the village of his ancestors to find peace. He'd bought the island of Kosmimo, which had once belonged to his family, from its Russian owner and founded a holistic resort which had been a success from the start. He'd also found happiness with Dell.

After landing in Athens, Claudia and Stefanos transferred to the helicopter that would take them to Kosmimo in the Ionian Sea, to the east of the island of Lefkada. Claudia had only once flown in a helicopter, on a holiday in New Zealand. It seemed surreal to fly by private jet and then by helicopter. But for Stefanos they seemed to be everyday modes of transport, scarcely worthy of mention.

The hour-long helicopter ride to Kosmimo was quite different from the smooth jet. The helicopter flew with a swooping motion, and either jerked sidewards or dropped suddenly if it encountered turbulence. And then there was the vibration...

Claudia battled nausea from the second she smelled the fumes of the fuel as they boarded. She and Stefanos wore headsets, to block the racket of the blades and to communicate with each other, but that made it only marginally better.

The only thing that took her mind off the nausea was her first sight of the small green island that looked like an emerald set in the multi-hued azure waters of the Ionian Sea. It was utterly beautiful. As the helicopter hovered above a helipad, preparing to land, she could see what looked like cleared farmland and, as they got closer still, white marble buildings interspersed with the aqua rectangles of swimming pools.

She couldn't help but feel a buzz of excitement. Pevezzo Athina was a luxury resort—the kind she had once dreamed of working at. She'd come close when she'd worked at a superb resort in Bali, but Pevezzo Athina had won so many international awards it was in a class of its own. How could she ever have imagined she would see it under these circumstances? And as a guest, not a member of staff?

'That's Alex and Dell down there, near the four-by-four, come to meet us,' Stefanos said through the headset. 'You'll like Dell. She's Australian, a foodie, and very warm and welcoming. She and Alex have two children—a little boy and a little girl.'

'I… I'm sure I will—like her, that is,' Claudia managed to force out through gritted teeth. She could scarcely talk, all her energy taken up with trying not to retch.

Her stomach lurched as the helicopter started its descent, flattening all the grasses and shrubs around it. And instead of arriving in style, meeting Stefanos's cousin and his wife with a confident smile, she had to be helped off the helicopter, taking care to stay out of reach of the blades.

Immediately she rushed to the cover of a bush, where she dry-retched until she could retch no more. She was left shaking and weak. Making an exhibition of herself again, she thought, as the helicopter took off.

'This…this is so humiliating,' she choked out to Stefanos, when she staggered back towards him from behind the bush. 'How can I face your cousin and his wife?'

'Not humiliating,' he said calmly. 'Natural for a pregnant woman, I believe.'

Her voice rose. 'I can't face them. Not like this.'

'Not much choice, I'm afraid. It's quite a walk

to my villa from the helipad.' He paused. 'No one will think any less of you. In fact, knowing my cousin and his wife, you will be bombarded with kindness. They're good people.'

She groaned. Without a word, he handed her a bottle of cool water to rinse her mouth and splash her face.

'Feeling better?' he said.

She nodded. 'Marginally. Thank you.'

The air smelt fresh and pure, with a hint of herbs and the tang of salt. She took a few deep breaths until the shakiness went away. But she was still grateful when Stefanos held her elbow as he steered her towards the car where Alex and Dell were waiting to greet them.

Dark good looks certainly ran in Stefanos's family—that was immediately apparent. And Alex was not only handsome, but charming in his greeting to her.

'*Kalosorizo*…welcome,' he said, with a big smile that had something of Stefanos in it.

Claudia liked him instantly.

Dell rushed to her side. Sweet-faced, auburn-haired, with kind olive green eyes. 'You poor thing—you must be feeling ghastly. I had morning sickness when I was pregnant with both my kids, and I remember only too well what it was like. But it doesn't last for ever. One day I woke up and felt fine—something to do with oestrogen levels, apparently. You'll see.'

'I certainly hope so,' Claudia said, attempting a weak smile.

'And it will be so worth it when you hold your baby in your arms.'

'I'm looking forward to that.'

Every time she thought of her baby it was with a rush of fierce, possessive love.

As Stefanos and Alex put Claudia's backpack in the car, Dell tucked her arm through hers.

'Stefanos did the right thing, bringing you here. Fresh air, healthy food—that is, when you can face food. The whole place is designed for guests to relax and revive. I'll personally devise a tempting pregnancy menu for you.'

'You're very kind,' Claudia murmured.

Again there was that sudden smarting of tears at Dell's thoughtfulness. Pregnancy was definitely an up-and-down journey.

Stefanos joined them. 'Straight to my villa for Claudia, I think,' he said.

Claudia was relieved. She was so exhausted that she didn't mind Stefanos taking over. In fact there was a certain comfort to it. 'I'm sorry,' she said. 'I know pregnancy isn't an illness, but after the helicopter flight I really don't feel wonderful.'

'Of course you don't,' said Dell. 'As soon as

Stefanos called I had your suite in his villa made up with fresh linen, and left a selection of organic crackers, fruit, and some ginger tea—which is very helpful for nausea,' Dell said. 'Your suite is ready too, of course, Stefanos. Later, you can both have dinner with us at our house, if you're up for it, or just order room service.'

Claudia was grateful for Dell's understanding. By emphasising the separate suites Dell was making it clear that she knew about the somewhat unusual situation with Claudia and her husband's cousin. She was grateful, too, to Stefanos. He had obviously told them the truth. She knew she couldn't have gone through the charade of pretending to be his fiancée or a long-time girlfriend.

The resort was a short drive from the heliport. Dell thoughtfully sat Claudia in the front seat of the car, with the window open and the breeze on her face. As they passed through the grounds Dell and Alex explained that they had always planned for Pevezzo Athina to be as self-sufficient as it could. They grew much of the fruit and vegetables for the resort, cultivated olives for olive oil, made cheeses, and had restocked the surrounding waters with fish. Renewable energy too.

'I'd love to know more,' Claudia said. 'I'm really interested.'

'Stefanos told us you had a background in hotels and hospitality?'

'That's true,' she said. 'But it's behind me now.'

For the first time she felt a real pang of sadness at the loss of her career.

She wondered what else Stefanos had told them about her?

Stefanos's villa was a white marble pavilion-style building, set around a courtyard with a swimming pool and an outdoor entertaining area shaded by a pergola covered with fresh green grapevines. A hot pink bougainvillea grew across the whitewashed wall in startling contrast.

'This is fabulous, Stefanos. What can I say?' she said as they stood by the pool after Alex and Dell had dropped them off.

'I can imagine you'll be spending some time lying in the shade around the pool and relaxing,' he said. 'Or I hope you will.'

She looked up at him. 'I'm not sick, you know. Just…hormonally incapacitated.'

He smiled. 'I realise that—but tell me you don't need a break.'

'I do need a break. You're right about that. And…and I'm grateful to you for bringing me to this heavenly place.'

Even though she wasn't quite sure how she

would be spending her time here—and knew that she needed to keep on her guard against him.

'My mother used to say to my father and I that on vacation we needed to wind down from stress and relax to the point of boredom.'

She smiled. 'I bet that didn't last long.'

'You're right. My father wasn't one for sitting around. He was energetic. We'd soon enough be sailing or hiking or skiing. Mama would more often than not come with us.'

'Energetic like you used to be?' she said. Then flushed as she remembered how very energetic they'd been together both back then and more recently. 'Er…can we go inside?'

The two main bedroom suites were set on either side of the courtyard. Between was a central kitchen, expansive living and dining areas, and a further two bedrooms with en suite bathrooms at the back. They were for extra guests, or if he wanted to bring his own staff, Stefanos explained.

His own staff. Again, she was struck by the differences in their worlds.

'Let me show you to your room,' he said. 'There are dark circles under your eyes.'

'Stop right there,' she said in mock command. 'I appreciate your concern, but you've already told me I look dreadful once today. It's not great for a girl's ego.'

He smiled. 'Even tired and nauseous you still look beautiful,' he said.

'That's better,' she said with a smile.

He might not mean it, but it sounded nice. She felt swept by an urge to hug him. Not with anything sexual in mind, but just because he was being kind. She hadn't expected he would want to please her—after all they meant nothing to each other now.

But ten years ago, in those passionate few months when they'd been together, he'd been not only her lover but her best friend—her *everything*. She had never imagined she would feel that way for a boy. She had never allowed herself to wonder how it might have ended if it hadn't been for that pregnancy scare and the awkward issues it had raised. That would have been far too painful. Although his ghosting had hurt, at the age of nineteen she had thought there would be other men like him—perhaps even better than him—in her future. How very wrong she'd been.

'Oh, my gosh, this is palatial—there's no other way to describe it,' she said, looking around her in delight.

The villa was all on one floor. All white, with white walls and marble floors, white linen and leather. Large windows with white shutters displayed views to the sea, which had white sails traversing across it, and out to the green hills behind the resort.

'It's so beautiful and peaceful,' she said.

'*Pevezzo* means safe haven in the local dialect,' he said.

'And Athina for the goddess Athina?'

'Or for Athens.'

'I think I'll go with the goddess rather than the city,' she said.

'It's also in honour of Alex's family's Taverna Athina, on a nearby island, and his grandfather's Athina restaurant in Sydney.'

'That's quite a link,' she said.

Stefanos showed her to her suite—a spacious bedroom, living area, bathroom and a small kitchen. The bed was enormous and looked very inviting, with a note of blue introduced into the white bed linens.

'If I can't rest and relax in here, I don't know where I could,' she said.

Images of what exactly she and Stefanos had done the last time they'd got within touching distance of a super-king-sized bed flashed before her. Thank heaven he had turned away from her and didn't see her blush.

'My suite is the mirror image of yours,' he said. 'I'll show you later.'

She felt an immeasurable relief. She looked

up at him. 'Thank you, Stefanos, for bringing me here. I can't imagine a more perfect place.'

'I think so too,' he said. He looked pleased.

'But how…how are we going to handle this? I mean, I don't expect you to hang out with me all the time. Are you actually going to stay here? Or will you go back to Athens?'

'I'm taking a vacation too. It's my favourite time of the year.'

It had been June when they'd first met in Santorini.

'It's a perfect time,' she said, unable to keep the wistfulness from her voice. This time around, life in June had become so much more complicated.

'As for how much time I spend with you—that's entirely your call,' he said. 'I can stay out of your way, if that's what you prefer.'

'No! I mean, I don't want you out of the way…'

But she had to play this carefully. There was a baby at stake here—*her* baby. And he was an all-or-nothing guy.

'Can we play it by ear?' she asked.

'Perhaps we could start with me showing you around tomorrow. There's something here in particular I think you'd like to see.'

Why did her mind stray to parts of *him* she'd like to see? It seemed that just because she was pregnant it didn't make her stop desiring him.

But that was just sex, nothing else, she had to remind herself.

'Er…that would be lovely,' she said.

'In the meantime, you should really eat something. Dell has left lots of stuff for you in the kitchen.'

'I'll shower first, and change,' she said.

'I'll be in the living room.'

Although she had the very best of intentions to join him, after a shower in the fabulous bathroom, surrounded by jets from all sides, Claudia changed into the thoughtfully provided white cotton pyjamas with the Pevezzo Athina logo in blue on the pocket and lay down on the bed… just for a minute. She closed her eyes…just for a minute.

When she woke it was well past dark, and she was alone in her beautiful room. A sheet was draped over her and she had vague memories of a deep, masculine voice as she was tucked in, a hand smoothing the damp hair from her forehead.

She must have imagined that he'd murmured, 'Goodnight, *koukla mou*.' Because that was the name he'd used to call her—a Greek endearment literally meaning *my doll*. But he would never call her that. He had never called her *koukla* again after she had refused his proposal. There was absolutely no way he would use that endearment now. It must have been a dream.

She got up and went in search of dry crackers.

CHAPTER ELEVEN

NEXT MORNING, CLAUDIA WOKE to the sound of soft splashing from the pool area and sun streaming through the shutters of her white bedroom in Stefanos's villa. She felt an immediate lifting of her spirits. Stefanos had brought her to a dream resort, and she was looking forward to exploring.

There was the familiar stirring of nausea, but thanks to Dell's supplies she was prepared. She sat up in bed and nibbled on the crackers she'd placed on the nightstand when she'd gone back to bed last night after a nocturnal snack. They were delicious—full of seeds and nuts. Would organic Greek crackers work better than the regular kind from a supermarket? She was prepared to believe it.

Feeling way better than she had when she'd arrived the previous afternoon, Claudia slipped into a simple white, embroidery-trimmed dress she'd bought in Bali, slid into leather flip-flops and headed out to the pool.

Stefanos was swimming. She stood in the shade of a grapevine and watched him as he streaked up and down the pool, his body as strong and true as an arrow, his even, rhythmical stroke barely breaking the surface of the water.

Her heart caught in her throat, arrested there by memories. She remembered all the times they'd swum together, diving with squeals of laughter from the deck of his boat into the aquamarine waters of the Aegean around Santorini. She hadn't been a confident swimmer when she'd first met him. Swimming in a chlorinated indoor pool for school lessons had never much appealed, although she'd enjoyed splashing around at the beaches in Devon. But, thanks to twenty-year-old Stefanos's help and encouragement, she'd soon been joyously swimming in the open sea with him, her lover.

She'd swum since on the Great Barrier Reef in Australia, among green turtles and baby sharks, in Bali among glorious coral and brilliant fish, and in New Zealand's Bay of Islands. She'd swum in so many different waters she should have forgotten where she'd learned to love open water swimming and who had taught her. But she never had forgotten. Never quite forgotten *him*.

He raised his head from the pool, his black hair wet to his head, droplets of water glistening on his tanned skin in the sunlight. He smiled that magnificent white smile and waved. She caught her breath as her heart tripped into overdrive. No other man had ever had the same effect on her. To be on holiday with him—yet not *really* be with him—was disconcerting, and it made her thoughts travel down pathways long blocked.

How could his appeal still be so strong? Back then it had surely been a fleeting first love— infatuation and sex and fun all wrapped into one all-encompassing emotion. It would have faded if it had run its course. What did she feel for him now? For the father of her baby? There was certainly something. Lust? Yes…oh, yes. Residual friendship? Who knew? Affection? Did she know this new Stefanos enough even to con- template growing fond of him? But he continued to surprise her in good ways. His kindness was unexpected, and yet she shouldn't be surprised. Even back then he'd been way more thoughtful than the usual twenty-year-old male she'd en- countered. When she'd told her university boy- friend she'd be away in Greece for a summer vacation he'd bluntly told her he wouldn't wait for her—typical behaviour for him.

But with Stefanos now, had that new dark layer of bitterness she'd identified in him smoth- ered his essential nature? Would he be capable of ruthlessly taking her baby from her? A shiver of dread ran through her. She would never let that happen.

'Are you coming in?' he called.

She shook her head. 'Not right now.'

With a few powerful strokes he was by the edge of the pool, looking up at her. 'Perhaps you'd rather swim in the sea?'

'That's a tempting offer,' she said.

'Shall we take a boat out before it gets too hot?'

'I would love that. Thank you.'

Effortlessly, he pulled himself up and out of the pool. His muscles rippled as he moved—they actually rippled—and she was struck speechless by the force of her attraction to him. An attraction she had to keep at bay. He had been wounded by his experiences with women since he'd known her. A wounded man could be dangerous…a man who could hurt her. Not physically—she didn't believe that of Stefanos for one moment. But he could hurt her emotionally. Especially when they had a child to bind them. Long gone was her naive belief that things in life would work out just because she really wanted them to.

Yet he was so impossibly hot, and she had to force herself not to stare at six foot two of virile, powerfully built Greek male, wearing nothing but brief swim-shorts, standing before her seemingly totally unaware of the effect he had on her. Being pregnant did not stop her from wanting him.

Thankfully he flung a towel around himself and her heartrate slowed back to normal.

'Dell sent over some food she thought might tempt you,' he said. 'She said she was able to keep down plain bread and cheese when she had morning sickness. She also suggests finely sliced peach and watermelon.'

'That's very thoughtful of her.' Claudia paused, looked up at him. 'Why is she being so nice to me?'

She had to remain on the alert. Did Stefanos have an ulterior motive in bringing her here? Was he manipulating her? If so, were Dell and Alex in on it?

'First of all because she seems to have taken to you…'

'And second?'

'You know the kind of married people who'd like to see everyone else paired off too? That's Dell and Alex.'

'But surely you've made it clear to them you're not interested in getting married? Er…getting married again, I mean.'

'Repeatedly. But they want to see me happy. Maybe they don't realise how unhappy a person can be within a marriage—or they've forgotten; Dell was married before.'

Back came the scowl that darkened his face when he mentioned marriage.

'They do know we scarcely know each other, don't they?' Claudia said.

What had he told them about her?

'They do. But they like you. And they didn't approve of my ex-wives.'

She needed to think about that one. He'd been so grim when he'd mentioned his matrimonial history before. 'When are you going to tell me about them? The ex-wives, I mean, who've made you so bitter,' Claudia said.

His jaw tightened. 'Don't you remember I told you I had no intention of discussing either of them?'

'I remember. But that was back then.'

He frowned. 'Why would that change?'

'Come on, it's kind of unfair to keep me in the dark when everyone else knows. It could get awkward. Imagine if I have lunch with Dell and she mentions one of them but I know nothing.'

A reluctant grin lifted the stern line of his mouth. 'You haven't changed at all, have you? If I don't spill you'll stage a relentless campaign until I do, won't you?'

'Maybe…' she said.

She needed to know so much more about this

man who was the father of her child. She wanted to be able to trust him. Right now, she wasn't at all certain she could, in spite of this unexpected trip to this fabulous place—or perhaps because of it.

He raised his eyebrows. 'Perhaps we can talk about them on the boat.'

'Sounds like a plan.'

Even more importantly, they needed to talk about how they would share their baby and how it would work.

'I'll think about it,' he said. He looked up at the perfect blue sky, which had just a few white clouds scudding across it. 'Conditions are perfect for sailing now, but there could be a storm later this afternoon. I know you want to see the resort, but I suggest we get out on the water first, then come back to the hotel for lunch. That is if Dell hasn't exhausted her supply of crackers.'

Claudia laughed. 'It's not fair to tease a pregnant woman. I might suddenly turn green on you.'

'Point taken,' he said, his grin still lingering. 'The resort is built on the top of a cliff. There's a road down to the dock but it's quite steep. Are you okay to walk or should I pick up a buggy?' Stefanos asked.

'I can walk. Just tell me they don't have donkeys here, like they use in Santorini for transporting tourists up the steep hill from the harbour.'

'No one here would countenance that, I can assure you.'

'Good,' she said. 'I'll go inside and get ready now.'

He went one way to his suite and she went the other to hers. She changed into gauzy white trousers and a cool, loose white shirt with boat shoes. Then she jammed on the white folding hat she always kept in her bag. As a redhead, she was always aware of striking a balance between enjoying the outdoors and protecting her skin from the sun. She managed to nibble on some bread and cheese, and packed up the rest to take on the boat.

The day before, Stefanos had told Claudia there was something he thought she might like to see. But he hadn't expected her to burst into tears at the sight of the *Daphne*, with her graceful lines and white sails, moored by the dock.

'You still have her after all this time! Your beautiful yacht!'

'She was a gift from my grandparents, named after my grandmother. I would never sell her,' he said. Even though, as an increasingly rare vintage model from a renowned designer, she was worth multiple millions.

Claudia fanned her face with her hand to excuse her tears. 'I'm sorry. Emotional…'

'Hormone disruption?' he said.

'Not just that, but it's that too, I suppose. It's just…it's like stepping through a portal into the past. I… I never thought I would see the *Daphne* again. Or you, for that matter. It…it brings back so many memories.'

'Not bad memories, I hope?' he said. Although he suspected he had left her with some bad memories.

'The very best of memories,' she said. 'Until… until right at the end.'

'We won't fast-forward to the end,' he said.

He had been so hot-headed, so stubborn, so determined to get his own way. And she had concealed information that might have made him less harsh towards her. Perhaps their ending could have been different. Or perhaps their passion for each other might have dwindled away with time, with distance, with other people… But knocking on the closed-off wall of his mind came a reminder about how quickly their passion had been reignited in London. He had to tread carefully.

She looked up at him, her blue eyes still misted with tears. 'I don't know if I can bear to get on board.'

'You don't have to if you don't want to,' he

said. Although he was disappointed at her reaction. Back then, she had loved the *Daphne*.

'I do want to. Or maybe I don't. I don't know... *Why?*' She gesticulated with her hands. 'Why are we back here together like this? How did it happen?'

'Fate, perhaps?'

'Fate?' she scoffed. 'You mean we had nothing to do with it?'

'The Ancient Greeks believed so strongly that fate governed our lives that we had not just one but three goddesses of fate.'

'Three?' she said.

'Sisters. Clotho, who spun each person's life thread, Lachesis, who measured how long that thread would be to give them their destiny, and Atropos, who cut the thread of life with her shears at the time of the person's death.'

'And you honestly believe that fate rules our lives?'

He shrugged. 'I can't discount it. Of all the people in London, why was it *you* who came to pack up my flat?'

'Coincidence?' she said.

'Why did you conceive, even though we used contraception?'

'Carelessness on our part? A fault in the manufacture?'

'All possibilities,' he said. 'Or I could choose to believe that you were fated to bear my child.'

Her eyes widened. 'That makes me sound like some kind of…of incubator. I don't know whether to be amused or offended.'

'Please don't be offended. I didn't mean it like that. I was just trying to answer your question of *why*. Don't think I haven't thought about why we've found ourselves in this situation.'

He'd thought of it constantly during the eight weeks they'd been apart after that day in Bloomsbury. He'd thought it might be fun to keep seeing her when he visited London, on a no-strings basis. He hadn't wanted anything serious, but he'd had too much respect for her to offer a pick-her-up-and-put-her-down kind of arrangement. And there had been a growing feeling that perhaps he shouldn't let her go. He didn't want marriage—neither did she. Perhaps they could have made something work…

But then she had called to inform him she was pregnant and everything had changed.

'Does there have to be a reason?' she said now. 'Couldn't it be coincidence?'

'Or luck?' he said.

'Luck?'

'Good luck that you came so unexpectedly back into my life,' he said. 'Good luck that you're pregnant with my baby when I had given up on any thought that I would be a father.'

'Good luck that I'm to be a mother when I hadn't chosen to be one? Good luck that I am deliriously happy about it?'

She paused, and he could read the emotions shadowing her face. She looked up to meet his gaze directly.

'I'm scared that you might try and take my baby from me,' she said. 'Would you do that, Stefanos?'

CHAPTER TWELVE

SHE HAD STUNNED him into silence. As Claudia looked up at Stefanos, where he stood opposite her on the boardwalk, his brow creased in what looked like sheer disbelief. Had she said the wrong thing? Had she wounded his feelings? But it had needed to be said.

'What do you mean?' he said slowly. 'You think I would take your baby?'

She gritted her teeth. 'I would hope not. But it's a possibility. You're so wealthy and I… I'm so not. I don't believe it's unheard-of for wealthy men to use their power to enforce sole custody. To not return children home from visits, to abduct them and…and take them to another country where the mother has no rights.'

'That might be true, and it's horrific,' he said gruffly. 'But I am not—would *never* be—one of those men.'

'I… I'd like to believe that, but—'

Stefanos put both his hands on her shoulders

and looked deep into her eyes. 'Claudia, please believe me, I would never take your baby from you. A child needs its mother.'

'I'm glad you think that.'

He seemed so sincere but who could know? She remembered how coldly he'd ghosted her... how cruel it had seemed.

'However, a child also needs its father,' he said seriously. 'I want to be a father to our child in any way I can.'

She narrowed her eyes. 'On whose terms would that be?'

'Terms? I was fortunate to have two good parents—as were you. I would hope for the same for our child. Visitation rights. Shared custody, if it comes to that. Financial support. Security. We need to sort out an agreement that's satisfactory to us both, in the child's best interests. It's early days. I only found out you were pregnant two days ago. You've had more time to get used to the idea of becoming a parent.'

He dropped his hands from her shoulders and stepped back. She missed his warmth, the connection. Even the most casual of contacts with him send awareness zinging through her. By confronting him, had she damaged the trust they'd seemed to be developing?

'What you've said is very reassuring,' she said. She was glad she'd brought the subject up. It had been nagging at her. Now it seemed her fears as to his intentions might have been completely off the mark. But there was still that doubt.

'And it's the truth,' he said.

'Stefanos, I want to believe you... I really do.'

He turned on his heel away from her, took a few steps and then came back. 'Do you honestly think I would abduct our baby and spirit him or her off to another country? Deny you your child?' He slowly shook his head. 'I look at the *Daphne* now and think of the two people we were then and wonder. How are we so very different?'

She swallowed hard against his anguish. 'The trouble is, we don't really know each other any more, do we?' she said. 'We had that glorious time together when I was a teenager, but we've known each other for only a few days since.'

'You're right. And in seven months' time we are going to be parents—independent of each other but joint in our care for our child. We each have to do our best for this baby who was—'

She put up her hand in a halt sign. 'Please don't call our baby an accident. That's a terrible label to give a child.'

'I was going to say unplanned—not an accident.'

'Good. Sorry. I'm glad. My twin sisters were never allowed to think they were in this world by accident. In fact they turned out to bring joy to all our lives.'

'We also have to do our best for each other, so we can be our best as parents,' he said. 'It's uncharted territory for us.'

He'd always had that grown-up side to him. Now, at thirty, he really was worldly wise. What he said made complete sense. Yet she felt an underlying sadness that two people who had conceived a child not in love, but in passion and respect, should be making such business-like arrangements for their child's upbringing and their separate participation in it. However— overwhelmingly—she was glad Stefanos wanted to be a part of her baby's life. That had turned out beyond her expectations. There were, she knew, many men who would deny all responsibility, all care, for a baby conceived from a one-day fling.

'Perhaps the best thing we can do is get to know each other all over again,' she said. 'As the people we are now...not the people we were back then.' She waved her hand towards the *Daphne*, symbol of their carefree past selves.

'Agreed,' he said, more quickly than she had expected him to. 'We have the next ten days to really get to know each other. A fresh start.' He held out his hand to shake. 'Deal?' he asked.

She shook his hand. 'Deal,' she said.

Long moments passed as she looked up at him, warmed by his smile and smiling back. This was a better outcome than she could have dreamed of.

'Now, do you remember how to help me cast off lines so we can set sail?'

'Remind me, and I'm sure it will all come back,' she said, still smiling.

Stefanos motored directly out in front of the resort. Claudia gazed back in admiration at the architecturally splendid white structures on the top of the cliff that formed the main part of the hotel. There were a series of other white buildings at the back. One of those larger buildings, set well away from the main complex, he explained, was the house Alex and Dell had built for their family. And quite a distance from everything else was a small white church.

'The views must be sensational from the front rooms of the hotel,' she said. 'No wonder it became so well known, so quickly.'

'Every room is sensational in its own way. Pevezzo Athina is magnificent at any time of the year. One year there was a family party here during the winter, and all the guests got snowed in for days. The island was cut off by rough seas and violent skies. I think they all enjoyed it.'

'It gets that cold here in the winter?'

'It doesn't snow every year—but, yes, it gets cold.'

'I think of the Greek islands as being eternally summer.' Like the eternal summer of her time with Stefanos, she thought wistfully.

Claudia helped him to raise the sails so he could navigate the *Daphne* around the island. With him at the helm, wearing white shorts and T-shirt—surely not the same shorts and T-shirt from ten years ago?—it was as if she'd stepped back in time to when she'd first been on his boat with him. Back then, she'd declared he'd had the best butt in Greece. She wouldn't say anything different now.

Only this time *he* was very different, *she* was very different, and the landscape around them was nothing like the volcanic ruggedness of Santorini and the smaller islands in the caldera.

Most of Kosmimo was heavily forested. Glorious waves of aquamarine and deepest blue lapped onto white sand beaches beneath white limestone cliffs, and the sun sparkled off the surface of the water. While the main beach formed part of the resort, there were smaller beaches along the coastline that were only accessible by boat.

'The hotel had been half constructed and then abandoned when Alex bought the island,' Stefanos explained. 'He finished it and added new buildings, working with architects from Athens.'

'What a project—and what a success,' she said. 'I can't wait to find out more about it... from a professional point of view, I mean.'

'Would you ever go back to your hotel career?' he asked.

'Never say never,' she said.

But her experience in Sydney had scarred her. Not just the duplicitous behaviour of the man she'd trusted, who had eroded her faith in other men, but her realisation that she might have been chasing a dream—a dream fuelled by her memories of her parents' pub in Devon, not the reality of working for multinational hotel operators. But she didn't regret it, and she'd loved having a job that let her travel.

'When did you buy your villa?' she asked.

'After my father died and I inherited,' he said. 'Alex was looking for investors, and he approached the family first. He's a few years older than me—we're related on my father's side through one of his sisters.'

'I wondered...there is a resemblance.'

Although, to her eye, Stefanos was the more handsome.

Not for the first time, she wondered what her baby would look like. Could she share that kind of discussion with Stefanos? He'd probably want to have some input into naming the baby. When would be too soon to discuss that?

She would have to be careful that such discussions didn't cross the line into a couples-type of intimacy that wasn't part of the arrangement. They might be going to be parents, but they weren't anything more than former lovers—although perhaps at the end of this holiday they might have formed a kind of friendship.

A pain as sharp as a stiletto pierced her heart at the thought of what they'd been to each other and how they had lost it. How would she explain to her child that he or she had both a mummy and a daddy, but Daddy lived in a different country and Mummy and Daddy didn't love each other?

'Alex and I became friends as adults, not as children,' Stefanos said.

'You were an only child—weren't you close to your cousins growing up?'

'Alex was older than me, and he lived in Australia. There were other cousins and family friends nearer to me in age, so I didn't lack companionship.'

She wondered why his mouth had tightened on the words *family friends.*

She dared to risk a question she'd wanted to hear answered since they'd first met again, back in his apartment in Bloomsbury. 'Tell me why you sold the shipping business. I remember, even after all this time, you telling me it was your destiny.'

'I did say that. It was. And in some ways I felt like I'd let my father and my late grand-father down by selling the business that was their hearts' blood. But it wasn't mine—never had been mine.'

'So why…?'

He looked straight ahead, his hands on the wheel. 'I wasn't always an only child. I had a brother—older than me by two years. He died when he was five years old of a childhood can-cer. I remember him… I was his little shadow, my mama says.'

'Oh, no. I'm so sorry, Stefanos. For your brother, for you, for your parents. Such a loss.'

'I sometimes dream of him as he might have been grown up. When I wake up, I feel the loss over again.'

'I'm sorry,' she said again, feeling how inade-quate her words were. To lose a child—a sibling—would be an unimaginable grief. She'd have to remain vigilant that, in spite of his reassurances, Stefanos didn't renege and take her baby away.

'Not only did I lose my big brother, I had to step up into the gap he'd left in the family. He would have been groomed for the business. I could have followed my own interests. I was always fascinated by the ancient history of my country.'

'How could you not be, growing up in Athens?'

'Not everyone shared my passion. And I wasn't destined to be an academic. How could I refuse to take on the mantle of heir to Adrastos Shipping? There were no other children to take it. My mother had suffered repeated miscarriages.'

Claudia gasped, and put her hand on her still-flat belly in an automatic reaction of protection. In her ninth week of pregnancy, she was still at the vulnerable stage.

'You can see why I want so much to take care of you,' he said.

'Yes, and I appreciate it even more now I know that,' she said. 'Fingers crossed my doctor will tell me everything is as it should be for a healthy pregnancy.'

Already, here in this beautiful place, on this glorious sea, she felt the tension, the stress and the worry starting to dissipate. Surprisingly, she wasn't feeling seasick—but then she had never been seasick, even in the roughest of seas.

Stefanos continued. 'There was always an obligation—unspoken, but very much there—for me to make up to my parents for the son they'd

lost…for the babies that were never born. I had
to be everything to them.'

'Did that seem like a burden?'

'Sometimes.'

She sensed a wealth of feeling behind that single word.

'Did you ever tell them you didn't want to go
into the business?'

'I was too dutiful to rebel. And there was
a lot at stake. My father had me working in
some capacity in the office from when I was
twelve years old—first in school vacations and
then university. I liked that. Believed I was part
of something. I felt grown-up and important,
even if I was only doing minor clerical jobs.
I was told that all work was vital to the company. At that age I wasn't aware of the scope of
the wealth Adrastos Shipping generated. But I
knew it had my name on it and would one day
be mine.'

'That was clever of your father.'

'I was indoctrinated at an early age,' he said
wryly. 'The summer I met you, I'd rebelled.
I'd had enough of working in my vacations. I
wanted the summer off. I took the *Daphne* to
Santorini to party with my friends.'

'Which you did,' she said. 'And you partied

with me too. Those were good times.' *The best of times.*

'There was another reason I chose Santorini for my vacation...'

'You mean apart from the fact it's one of the most desirable destinations in the Mediterranean?'

'I also wanted to visit the archaeological dig at Akrotiri. It's the remains of a sixteenth-century BC city, incredibly well preserved in volcanic ash. So much is still there of the life the Minoan people lived before the volcano blew out the centre of their island. They had drainage systems, and they traded using pottery to hold oils and wine, just like we use today, painted incredible frescoes... I'm fascinated by it as a record of an advanced civilisation at a time when much of the world was in the Stone Age.'

'When did you visit Akrotiri?' she asked, curious that he had never mentioned this when they'd been together.

'Before I met you at the bar. And again when you were at work.'

'You never told me about your interest in archaeology. Or your work at the shipping company and your rebellion that year.'

'The archaeology had become a hidden passion I didn't talk about. And when it came to

Adrastos Shipping, I didn't want to identify my job as my life.'

'Seems like we were both wearing masks of some kind that summer,' she said slowly.

CHAPTER THIRTEEN

STEFANOS FOUND IT almost impossible to stop admiring Claudia in her swimsuit. It was a modest one-piece, a serious swimmer's suit, in a swirl of blues that complemented her fair skin and bright hair, showed off long, slender legs.

Her body had changed. Her stomach was still flat, but her breasts definitely looked larger. For all their civilised talk of custody and support, he felt the raw truth hit him. The miracle of it. Inside her body she was growing their baby—a *person*. Someone who would become a child, a teenager, an adult—a member of his family. *An Adrastos*. He didn't want to miss out on any of that. Hell, he didn't want to miss out on seeing her body changing and growing. A fierce surge of possessiveness hit him. Not just for his baby, for *her*.

'Yes, my breasts have grown,' she said teasingly.

'You weren't meant to notice me looking,' he

said, disconcerted at being caught out and by the fact that she'd called him on it.

'I'm quite impressed myself,' she said. 'They've never been on the generous side.'

Her breasts were perfect. Everything about her was perfect. *She* was perfect. As perfect as an imperfect human being could be. But could he trust his own judgement any more on what was perfect and what wasn't? What if he got it wrong again?

Claudia fitted her goggles. 'Are you coming in?'

He had anchored the *Daphne* within easy swimming distance of a small, postcard-pretty beach with a curve of white sand and a limestone cliff towering behind.

'Yep,' he said, picking up his own goggles.

She moved to dive from the edge of the boat, as he'd seen her do so many times in the past. But he covered the distance between them in two quick steps and grabbed her by the arm. 'Wait,' he said. 'Should you be diving from a height straight into the water? You know…because you're pregnant?'

Claudia started, shocked. 'I… I probably shouldn't.' She tore off her goggles. 'How stupid of me. I didn't give it a thought.'

Tears misted her eyes. He thought the hormones must be playing up again, but didn't dare say so.

'Not stupid. And I thought about it in time to stop you. So no need to worry.'

'I want to do everything right for the baby.'

'You *are* doing everything right,' he reassured her.

'But I didn't even think about diving.' Her voice rose, then broke. 'I… I've got a library of pregnancy books. I must have flicked over the chapter about swimming because at the time there wasn't any possibility I'd be in a Greek paradise, diving off the side of a yacht.'

She seemed to crumple, and he realised again how vulnerable she was. He took her into his arms in a hug. And realised it was exactly where he wanted her to be.

'It's understandable. When your bump gets bigger you probably won't even think about diving. Besides, there's two of us here to think about such things.'

'It's sweet of you to say so, but I know you're only trying to make me feel better.'

Her voice came muffled, from against his shoulder, and he felt a shudder that might have been a poorly disguised sob.

'Is it working?' he asked.

'It is.' She sniffed. 'I do feel better. Not only just now…since you helped me pack my bag and spirited me away from London. Since you made me feel better about staggering off a helicopter and retching in front of people I didn't know. The fact I'm here at all is because you're looking after me. I… I don't feel so alone. Thank you.'

Stefanos tightened his arms around her. There was only the thin fabric of her swimsuit between them. He was bare-chested, in just swim-shorts. He didn't want to let her go. She felt so good there—as if she were reclaiming her place by his side from before, when they'd been together.

As the water slapped gently against the side of the boat, black-headed gulls wheeled above them, and silvery fish rose to the surface, he held her close. He felt her heart beating against his chest, marvelling that another little life was there too. *His child.* When were you able to hear the baby's heartbeat? Would Claudia let him come with her to her doctor's appointments? Would she trust him enough?

She pulled away and leaned back against the circle of his arms so she could look up into his face. Their gazes met and he looked into her eyes for a long moment. He didn't know what he was searching for, but he had an overwhelming feeling that one day he would find it there. She smiled, a slow, tremulous smile, and as he dipped his head to kiss her mouth she reached up to meet him. Her lips parted under his, warm and pliant and welcoming. It wasn't a passionate kiss—not yet. Although the potential was always there when he was this close to Claudia. It was tender, affirmative, acknowledging something he could no longer deny.

'You know I haven't ever stopped being attracted to you?' she murmured against his mouth, her voice not quite steady.

'Nor me you,' he said. 'I can't imagine I would ever stop being attracted to you. Even if I fought it.'

She kissed him again—slowly, tenderly, almost pretty.

'I have fought it and it wouldn't go away,' she said. 'I've never felt for anyone the way I felt for you. It made me angry with myself—that I'd let a teenage crush hold me back, stop me from giving other people a chance. Eventually I talked myself out of it. Or thought I did. Then, when I saw you again in Bloomsbury... Well... you know what happened.'

'It was the same for me. Instant. All-encompassing. Only this time there are consequences. Something that could spin us apart. Or focus us together.'

'Is talking like this part of us getting to know each other again?' she said.

'I believe it could be,' he said.

'Almost...almost like dating?'

'We didn't date as such in Santorini,' he said.

'There was nothing gradual about it back then. We fell straight into a relationship.'

A relationship he'd thought would be for life.

'We went from hello to head-on with nothing in between,' she said.

How exhilarating that had been. No feeling had ever come close to the crazy tumble of falling in love with her. And his attempts to find it again had ended in unmitigated disaster. Perhaps because he was fated not to be with anyone else but Claudia?

He didn't put forward that idea, anticipating a scathing reaction from her. He was not too sure how he felt about it himself—it could be a trap he fell into.

'Shall we start dating now?' she said.

'Ten years after I spotted a gorgeous, laughing redhead in that bar in Santorini?'

'Why not?' she said.

'For our first date, would you care to join me for a swim? Followed by a snack of dry bread?'

She laughed. 'I couldn't think of anything better.'

From the ladder at the side of the *Daphne*, Claudia pushed herself safely into the unbelievably clear aquamarine sea. The water embraced her and refreshed her, the perfect temperature. She turned around to watch Stefanos execute a perfect dive into the water and emerge next to her.

'This is heaven,' she said. 'Absolute heaven.'

She duck-dived below the surface, marvelling at the light coming down in shafts through the different tones of turquoise, illuminating the white sand, the water plants waving in the current, the small brighty coloured fish darting between the rocks, and a red starfish. She would like to snorkel here. Did the resort stock snorkelling gear? she wondered. Stefanos had taught her to snorkel in Santorini.

She emerged to swim parallel to the beach, Stefanos keeping pace beside her.

'There must have been good beaches in Sydney,' he said, when they paused to tread water and look around.

'There were amazing beaches. But I was always a bit nervous in the water…about sharks and stinging things.'

'No sharks here,' he said. 'But keep an eye out for the occasional jellyfish. And when we get close to shore don't step on any sea urchins.'

She'd forgotten how protective he could be. Not possessive, but nurturing and encouraging. For the first time she let herself imagine what kind of father Stefanos would be. And then lost the thought when he challenged her to a race to the beach.

Once she'd dried off in the warm mid-morning sun, Claudia decamped to the shade of a group of small fresh-scented pine trees growing at the edge of the sand. Stefanos joined her. She sat with her arms wrapped around her knees. He picked up a stick and doodled circles with it in the sand.

'Please tell me we can swim here every day,' she said. 'I absolutely love it.'

'Here, or one of the other beautiful beaches of Kosmimo. If you like, we can sail to the other islands, or to Nidri for its shops and restaurants. There are some family-run tavernas on the smaller islands accessible only by boat.'

'Like the ones we went to in Santorini?'

'The same. Do you remember that taverna on the water, where you fed all your barbecued sardines to the stray cats?'

She laughed. 'And you pretended to be cranky, but kindly let me share your lunch.'

'I wasn't pretending to be cranky.'

'Yes, you were. I noticed you feeding some of your sardines to the poor, hungry little cats too. You just wouldn't admit it.'

'I will neither confirm nor deny the truth of that,' he said very sternly, although a grin played at the corners of his mouth.

'But I remember the truth,' she said.

'I'm surprised you remember so much about those times.'

'You do too,' she said.

'Yes,' he said.

But did he remember it like she did? How they'd spent so much time making love? How they'd laughed at the same things?

'But can you not mention sardines again? My lurking nausea doesn't like the idea of them. Urgh…'

He laughed. 'Forget I ever said that word.'

A long silence fell between them. An iridescent dragonfly landed on her foot and she held her breath until it flew away. Wasn't a visit from a dragonfly a portent of transformation and change? If you believed in such things, of course.

She turned to him. 'What happened with your ex-wives?'

He groaned. 'I might have known you wouldn't let go of that.'

'You knew I wouldn't,' she said, with a laugh.

But she was very serious. What had happened in the last ten years to make him so bitter, so anti-marriage, when back then he'd been so keen on it? She hadn't changed *her* views on marriage—not after having held on to her independence for so long.

She shuddered when she remembered how she had weakened in her long-held stance of not letting a man come before her career and allowed Brad to dominate and manipulate her. Perhaps she'd been so vulnerable to him because she'd been lonely in Sydney. Whatever the reason, she'd been blind to the fact he was a con man of the first order. But if she'd married a man like that, not knowing what he was, she would have been trapped. Of course there had been no chance of that with Brad because, unbeknownst to her, he'd already been married.

No, she was no more open to marriage than she had been at nineteen. And even if she had changed her mind, was a man with two ex-wives a good bet as a husband? But he was the father of her child. She needed to know what had made him the man he was now.

'If it was a real first date surely you wouldn't ask me about my ex-wives,' he said.

'Technically, I asked you before we went on this date.'

He sighed a deep, heartfelt sigh that almost made her feel sorry for him. *Almost.*

'Start with wife number one,' she suggested.

'Right. Wife number one,' he said, and snapped the stick he'd been doodling with in half. He looked at the two broken pieces but didn't say anything further.

'Her name?' she prompted.

She needed to hear what had happened to him,

but at the same time she felt a sick dread. Because she could not bear the thought of him with any other woman but her. Even though she had initiated this conversation, she wanted to put her hands over her ears.

'Arina,' he said. 'She was my mother's god-daughter, a family friend, a childhood playmate.'

So that was why that shadow had darkened his eyes at the words 'family friends'.

'So you'd known her all her life?'

'That's right—although I hadn't seen her for some years while she was away at university. Then she started an internship at an Adrastos Shipping supplier and we were thrown together again. I was devastated by losing my English girlfriend—'

'Me?'

'Who else?' he replied curtly, with an edge to his voice that cut. He tossed the broken sticks away from him down the sand. 'Little did I know Arina was suffering heartache of her own. Also, both sets of parents, for reasons of their own, were pushing us together. Arina was—is—a sweet person. Whether she was saying what she thought I wanted to hear, or genuinely believed it, she told me that above all she wanted a family. Her words were a balm to my wounded pride after your rejection. Before I knew it we were married. We were both twenty-two. It was a disaster for both of us. I got a wife who seemed to see the marital bed as a duty to be endured or evaded.'

Now Claudia really did want to cover her ears.

'And she got a husband who couldn't be what she wanted.'

'Why was that?' Claudia asked, not sure she really wanted to hear the answer.

'Because, to put it bluntly, I was the wrong sex. She'd been in love with her best friend— her chief bridesmaid at our wedding—since they were at school. But her family was ultra-conservative.'

'So she couldn't come out as her true self. Poor Arina. That's very sad. I wonder if her parents hoped marriage to you would "cure" her.'

'Something like that. Her story has a happy ending. Six months after our wedding she left me for her friend, who felt the same way about her. They're very happy. I went to their wedding. Arina and I are friends now—of a sort.'

'But you hold a grudge?'

'Because of the dishonesty. I was lied to by her, by her family, even by my own mother— who was hoping marriage would be the best thing for Arina—and by my father because he saw it as a strategic marriage between the heirs to two major shipping companies.'

'That was a lot to bear on your shoulders.'

And she'd bet it had been a blow to his masculinity—to be left for a woman.

'I didn't want there to be lies about the reason for the break-up, and neither did Arina and her wife. We told the truth and eventually the wave of scandal ebbed away.'

'And left you lying shattered on the shore?'

'That's one way of putting it,' he said. He took a deep breath. 'Both the marriage and its aftermath were hell. How could I ever trust again?'

'I'm sorry it turned out so rotten for you. But it's nothing you can be blamed for.'

No wonder he was wary.

'Marriage number two was even worse.' He cradled his head in his hands in a gesture of despair. 'I really don't want to relive that time. It was brutal.'

'Then don't,' Claudia said, alarmed. She reached out a hand to rub his back in silent comfort. 'Please. Forget I asked.'

He raised his head to face her and she dropped her hand. 'You'll only ask me again later, now your curiosity's aroused.'

'Of course I won't. Not if it upsets you.' She paused. 'Maybe I will ask you again. But you don't have to tell me now.'

He groaned in mock surrender. 'Now I've started, I might as well finish.'

'Only if you feel comfortable. Seriously. It was obviously very painful for you.'

'This is for the last time, okay? We won't speak of it again.'

'Okay.' She felt guilty that she was stirring up bad memories. But she had to know. His marriage mistakes could impact on her child's future. And she also wanted to know for her own sake. She'd be lying if she denied that.

His face set in grim lines. 'I met Tiana at a big annual yacht show in the South of France when I was twenty-seven. It's an international trade show for superyachts.'

'Wait. You were twenty-seven? Hadn't you sold the shipping company by then?'

'All but the yacht charter division, which is lucrative and has always interested me. I've doubled the business since.'

He might be an archaeologist in his heart but he was a billionaire in his blood, Claudia thought.

'So you met her at the yacht show...' Another indication of his elite world, inhabited by the richest of the rich.

'I should have known better. There are people there from all around the world. Not everyone is who they say they are at such an event.'

'And she wasn't?'

Again, she felt uncomfortable to think about

him with another woman. But it was in his past, the experience had shaped him, and he had already flagged that it hadn't ended well. She had to grit her teeth and listen. After all, she'd asked him.

'She was glamorous, fun, just what I needed at that time. I didn't expect her to end up in Athens, but she did on some believable pretext. What I didn't realise was that she'd targeted me, researched me and hunted me down.'

'Surely not?'

Yet he was a billionaire, and quite a prize for the kind of person who went after such a trophy. Again, she began to see why he might be bitter and reluctant ever to commit again.

'My mother had a name for her: *chrysothiras*, which translates as gold-digger. But of course I didn't believe her.'

'And was she? Tiana, I mean? A gold-digger?'

'A gold-digger extraordinaire. She knew exactly how to play me. I was snared before I knew it. I thought I was marrying a caring woman who wanted a family as much as I did. But by accident I found out she was older than she'd said, and had a child hidden away with her parents—who she'd told me were dead—and no interest in having more children. Everything was a lie.'

'Stefanos, I can't believe it… Why would she do that?'

'Money.' His voice was blunt with betrayal.

'I hope she didn't get any.'

'Enough to get her out of my life for ever.'

'I'm so sorry you had to go through that. You do know, though, don't you, that you are worth so much more than money? You're handsome, intelligent, kind—'

He brushed her words away. 'And a terrible judge of women. I will never, ever take that risk again. There won't be a marriage number three. Thanks to you, I will have a child in my life, but I don't want a wife.'

She couldn't blame him for being so vehement.

'Those two divorces were hardly typical,' she said. 'You've had very bad luck. Many of us make our mistakes without actually marrying them.'

'Like you did?'

She paused. 'If you want to hear my unedifying story, I suppose I'll have to share. It's not pretty. You might think less of me when you hear it.'

'I very much doubt that. Let's hear it. On the proviso that we never talk about past mistakes again.'

'Agreed,' she said wholeheartedly. 'I was a real mug. Do you know that expression?'

'Someone who's deceived, made a fool of?'

'That was me. I was made to look a real sucker by Brad.' She gritted her teeth. 'I still cringe when I remember how it panned out. I can't bear to think about how blinkered I was.'

Now it was Stefanos's turn to lay a comforting hand on her shoulder. 'It's not a good feeling.'

'Here goes,' she said, putting her hand over his. 'I was working in a hotel in Sydney. It was in a fabulous spot—right on the harbour. Brad was my boss. Usually I wouldn't go out with someone I worked with, but I only knew a few people there and he was very persuasive. He soon had me hooked. I didn't know he was getting my signature on documents that were contracts for supplies from companies owned by members of his wife's family. Yes, his wife—who I didn't know existed. Turned out she had no idea I existed either, and she wasn't aware of the deals Brad was doing with her brothers. She reported him and me for fraud. It got nasty. The press picked up on the "love triangle", which was further humiliation. I had to fight to clear my name—which I eventually did, at considerable expense and anguish. The shine was already wearing off the hotel business for me, and that completely tarnished it. That's when I went back home to the UK, with a firm resolve that I would never let myself get caught like that again.'

'You weren't dealt a fair hand.'

'No. But I ended up with my own business, so perhaps it wasn't such a bad hand. I don't have to answer to a man for anything.'

'And that business led you back to me...'

'And now I'm having a baby—which is happy news for both of us.' She took a deep breath. 'Stefanos, I'm sorry I couldn't be what you needed back then. But I'm glad that in an unconventional, roundabout way you're getting something of what you wished for—a child.'

'And you still say you don't believe in fate?' he said.

CHAPTER FOURTEEN

STEFANOS RELAXED BACK into his chair at the table in the hotel restaurant where, after their swim, he and Claudia had met Alex and Dell for lunch. He marvelled at how instantly Claudia had got on with his cousin and his wife, with her warm laugh and easy, informed conversation. She fitted in as no other woman he'd introduced to them ever had.

She talked all the talk—about hotels and hospitality, travel around Asia, her thoughts on Sydney, Alex and Dell's hometown, as well as on babies and children. Not only that, she talked the talk in Greek *and* English. As they'd sat down at the table she'd announced she wanted to practise and get her language skills back. She was doing well—soon she'd be back to the fluency that had seen her bantering back and forth with the customers in that Santorini bar so long ago. He felt inordinately proud of her.

He contributed to the conversation when required. Of course he had to tell the story of how Claudia had suddenly appeared from his past, to pack up his apartment for his move back to Athens. How they'd reconnected. How—obviously—they'd got on very well indeed. How they were taking it day by day in terms of a renewed friendship.

'Did all the old attraction come rushing back when you first saw her?' Dell asked.

'Yes,' he said.

That was the polite response, but it was also the truthful one. That old attraction was churned up with bitterness and blame, but it was still there, strong as it had ever been. Thoughts of how their morning together had been an echo of earlier times, when they'd been everything to each other, kept intruding. But he didn't want to get married, and neither did she. How could they make that work to result in something mutually beneficial?

When he'd got back to Athens he had texted her, suggesting a meeting in London, intending to have the same kind of conversation he'd had with her on the *Daphne* this morning—to suggest they get to know each other again with no pressure for commitment on either side. The baby had put an entirely different slant on it. Others seemed to be putting an urgency on the nine-month countdown that he and Claudia did not.

Dell was obviously dying to know the details of what had happened in London, and he wondered if Claudia would share them with her. He hoped not. Their encounter might have been what some would call a 'one-morning stand', but making love with Claudia had always been special and private to him, and that time together had been no different. Dell wouldn't be getting the details from *him*, that was for sure.

Alex and Dell had not got on with either of his ex-wives. Arina had been awkward with Alex—Dell hadn't been on the scene then—in the way of someone hiding a deep secret. And after he'd split with Tiana, Dell had made no bones about how much she'd disliked and distrusted his glamorous older wife.

'Frankly, she was the kind of person where you'd count the silver after she'd been in the room,' Dell had said.

That had only made him feel worse about his massive error of judgement in marrying Tiana. He'd beaten himself up about it ever since. But he felt better about those disastrous marriages now, after his conversation with Claudia on the beach. He'd had very bad luck, she'd said, putting a different and more forgiving slant on it. He'd married his mistakes, she'd said.

Maybe it wasn't such an irrevocably shameful thing to be twice divorced before thirty when you looked at it that way. But it still made him dead against marrying another 'mistake'. And he was being not so subtly pushed towards marriage by his cousin and his wife. They'd made their approval of Claudia very obvious.

'She already seems like part of the family,' Dell joked, but narrowed her eyes to see his reaction.

When his mother found out about Claudia's pregnancy the pressure would really be on. But Claudia also had reasons to resist marriage— she had made that very clear. These days, pregnancy was no reason to get married. He was determined he and she would sort out access and time spent together without interference from his family, no matter how well-meaning.

He noticed that Claudia was eating very little. 'You okay?' he asked quietly.

She nodded. 'Just being careful. I'm actually feeling much better.'

'The swim did you good,' he said.

She leaned towards him to murmur in his ear, so that only he could hear. 'So did being with you.'

She then turned away to talk to Dell, and he was left wondering if he had misheard her.

After the meal, he headed back to the villa

to make some calls while Dell gave Claudia a grand tour of the resort. He was surprised at how empty his villa seemed without her, though she hadn't spent even twenty-four hours there. Her presence was there in the flip-flops left outside the door, the linen jacket draped on the back of a chair, a hint of her floral perfume in the air. Oh, and those dry crackers and the scent of ginger tea.

He was in the living area, talking on his phone, when Claudia got back, flushed and excited after her tour of the resort. Stefanos immediately ended the call to greet her.

She was bubbling. 'Stefanos, this place is even more wonderful than I had imagined! It has to be the best resort I've seen. Better even than that heavenly place in Bali. Better than Bay Breeze, my favourite place near Sydney—which, it turns out, is owned by Alex's friends the Morgan brothers. Dell helped put it on the map when she was a food writer. Pevezzo Athina just excels in every way. Of course the location is superlative, and the views priceless, but the white marble buildings, the luxury of the fit-outs, the grounds, the holistic approach, the level of service—everything. This place deserves every accolade and award it's been given.'

She flung herself on the sofa beside him.

'Thank you, thank you, thank you for bringing me here.' She planted a kiss on his cheek before kicking off her boat shoes and throwing herself back against the sofa. 'Trouble is, I'll never want to leave.'

Why did she have to? She could live here. Help his cousin run the resort if that was what would please her. He was sure it would please them. Surely that would beat packing boxes? And it would be so much easier for him to visit his child here than it would be to go from Athens to London. It seemed a perfect solution. But it was early days yet to mention it to Claudia.

'I'm glad you like it so much.'

'You were smart to invest,' she told him.

'Yes,' he said.

His father had also made an initial investment, as had Alex's other cousin Cristos. It had indeed proved to be a smart move.

'But my feet are killing me,' she went on. 'I didn't realise they would swell in the heat. Dell said it happened to her when she was pregnant too.' She wiggled her toes and rotated her ankles.

'Here, let me,' he said, taking her pale, slender feet in his hands. He massaged her ankles, her feet, between her toes.

'Oh, that's so much better,' she said, closing her eyes, sighing her appreciation. 'Oh, yes. Harder. That's lovely. Mmm... Don't stop.'

She was making the same moans of pleasure as she did when they made love…

Claudia lay back against the sofa and gave herself over to the bliss of Stefanos massaging her feet with his big, strong hands. He had a magic touch. It felt so good. Mmm…

Perhaps too good.

Abruptly she sat up and swung her feet over the edge of the sofa. 'Thank you, that really helped.' She wiggled her feet. 'Much better.'

'I don't have to stop.'

His voice was deep and husky and she knew exactly what he meant. Because her thoughts had run along exactly the same sexy track.

'Yes. You do. If you don't stop, the next thing we'll be making love on the sofa.'

He grinned a lazy grin that chipped away at her resolve. 'Would that be such a bad thing?'

'Not a bad thing—of course not a *bad* thing. But…but an unwise thing. We might only have one chance to get this shared parenting thing right. Making love raises the stakes…makes it more difficult for me to think straight. I know it's different for men, but for me sex is more than just physical, it's emotional. And the more invested I am, the more…well, the more vulnerable I am.'

The more in danger she was of falling in love

with him all over again. The more in danger of being hurt when they went back to their separate lives.

'What makes you think it's different for men?'

She shrugged, as if no explanation was required. 'Well… Men.'

He frowned. 'That's an unfair generalisation. Some men, perhaps. Not this man.'

'I'm sorry if I got that wrong.' She remembered how he had worshipped her, looked into her eyes while they made love.

'You're forgiven,' he said.

But had he forgiven her for how she'd hurt him ten years ago?

'The idea of us "dating" is that we get to know each other slowly,' she said.

'In Santorini we went to bed together that first night.'

'My point precisely. And then we realised we didn't know each other as well as we thought we did. Perhaps didn't know each other as well as we needed to when we hit a barrier.' She paused, planted a quick, fierce kiss on his mouth. 'That doesn't mean I don't want you. Because I do. Badly.'

He groaned and sat back further away from her on the sofa. 'Don't say that. Knowing you want me as much as I want you only makes it worse.'

'It does for me too—believe me. But we don't have just us to consider now. There's our baby. And the better the relationship is between us, the better it will be for him or her.'

'How can I argue with that?' he said.

'Talking about the baby...can I ask you something?'

'As long as it's not to stop wanting you, because I can't,' he growled.

She laughed. 'No. Not that. Would you like to be involved in my pregnancy? Come along with me to my first scan, for example? It's done at around twelve weeks and it's called "the dating scan". It's to check that everything is developing okay and to confirm how far along I am in the pregnancy so they can calculate the due date.'

'I would very much like to be there,' he said.

He sounded pleased—that was a first step. She was glad. She genuinely wanted him to be there. There was also another motive—if she involved him, showed him what a meticulously caring mother she intended to be, that would be a defence against any later attempt by him to undermine her. Not that she really thought that might happen, but she had to consider it.

'Of course I know exactly the day this baby was conceived, because it was only the once with you. I mean it wasn't just the once—it was more

than once…more than twice—but the one day…
you remember.'

'Oh, yes, I remember,' he said.

'Being pregnant and single isn't…well, it isn't
as easy as I thought. Medical people keep asking
about the father and I don't know all the answers—
like I didn't know your blood group and it was
important. It's all so exciting, but it's a bit lonely.
There are some things I want to share.'

'Give me notice and I'll be there. I'll come
from Athens. Thank you for not locking me out.'

She was surprised he might have felt locked
out. But perhaps she had been so fearful of him
taking her child that that was exactly what she
had done.

'Do you have any questions?' she asked.

'When can we hear the baby's heartbeat? That
will be a reassuring thing to hear.'

'I think we'll hear it at the ultrasound scan.'

'Are you aware of it now?'

'Not at all,' she said. 'I'm looking forward to
hearing a heartbeat too.'

He got up from the sofa. 'I've got more questions—but first can I get you a drink or some
more crackers? By the way, are your feet still
hurting? If so, why not put them up on some
cushions? I'll stack them for you.'

'The cushions are a good idea—why don't I
stack them while you get us that drink.'

Had he been this thoughtful when he'd been twenty? Looking back, she thought he probably had. Only she had taken it for granted. Perhaps she needed to trust him now.

'Entaxei,' he said. Okay.

Comfortable on the sofa, her feet elevated on a stack of cushions and a Greek lemon drink recommended by Dell in her hand, Claudia returned to their conversation.

'What other questions do you have?'

'When can they tell you the sex of the baby?'

'I haven't asked because I don't want to know. Old-fashioned of me, I suppose, but I'd like it to be a surprise.'

'I'm good with that,' he said. 'I don't care what the sex is, as long as it's healthy.'

'As long as it's healthy,' she said at the same time, and they laughed. 'That said, if tests need to be done that reveal the sex, I couldn't bear for the medical staff to know and not us.'

'Agreed,' he said.

'I wonder what our baby will look like?' she mused.

'With you a fair-skinned redhead and me with black hair and olive skin, who knows?'

'I reckon your colouring will dominate. Your hair is so very black.'

'It might. But there are some blondes in my family. And some green eyes.'

'Another surprise for us,' she said. 'Have you thought about names? I believe there's a lot of naming traditions in Greek families.'

These were all the things she'd wanted to discuss with him but hadn't dared.

'Traditionally, a first son is named after the father's father, and the first daughter after the father's mother. Then the second son is named after the mother's father and the second daughter after her mother.'

'As we're not married, would that be expected?' she said.

'I don't see why,' he said. 'Sometimes a grandparent's name is used as a second name.'

'Were you named after your grandfather?'

'Yes.'

'What are your parents' names?'

How little she really knew about him.

'My mother's name is Dimitra and my father is Vasileios.'

'Dimitra is pretty, but I'm not so sure about your father's name.'

'I like it because I loved my father. But we don't have to stick with any of those traditions. After all, we're not following convention, and of course you're not Greek. Perhaps our child deserves its own name.'

'I'll think about it at another time,' she said, taking the ball back into her own court.

'Do you want our baby to be bilingual?' he asked.

'Absolutely. I'll talk to him or her in both languages. For one thing, when he or she goes to visit you in Greece, they'll need to be able to speak Greek.'

Claudia was beginning to find this subject painful—their separateness, their child going back and forth between them. A future with Stefanos in it only at designated times and meeting places. Good for the child, but not so good for her to hear it put in such matter-of-fact terms.

Because so many times today she'd been reminded of just why she had fallen so deeply in love with Stefanos.

CHAPTER FIFTEEN

STEFANOS COULDN'T IMAGINE a moment more perfect than this: swimming with Claudia around one of the small uninhabited islands near Kosmimo. The *Daphne* was anchored on the other side of the island in perfectly calm seas as they swam the island's perimeter. There was no other boat or person in sight. Just him and Claudia together in the warm, buoyant sea under the most perfect blue summer morning sky.

He was a strong swimmer, but she matched him, her stroke graceful, her body sleek and strong, as they speared through water that ranged from midnight-blue to sparkling turquoise. Shafts of sunlight illuminated the white sand of the sea floor, shoals of tiny fish darted around them, and small ghostly white jellyfish pulsed away with their stinging tentacles wafting behind them.

Claudia tapped him on the arm. 'Look up on the cliffside.'

She trod water, drops of salt water glistening on her shoulders like crystals, and Stefanos looked up to see five small, shaggy wild goats defying gravity as they effortlessly scaled the sheer vertical surface.

'Never fails to amaze,' he said.

'How on earth do they get up there without falling off?'

'Their hooves are very hard on the outside, so they can dig into the tiniest of ledges, and they have soft, cushiony pads below, which mould to the wall like a natural climbing shoe. Those goats are sturdy and agile. They have been a part of this landscape for a very long time, and their ancestors played an important role in Greek mythology.' He stopped. 'You probably don't want a lecture on that.'

'But I do—it's fascinating. Tell me more.'

'Zeus, the king of the gods, was hidden as a baby from his father Cronus, who wanted to destroy him because he would eventually dethrone him. He was given shelter by a goat named Amaltheia, who nourished him as a foster mother. Her horn became the cornucopia—the horn of plenty. There are other myths about goats going back thousands of years. And they're depicted on a lot of ancient art.'

Claudia looked up at the goats with something akin to reverence. 'It's a privilege to see them.'

She waved her arms around her. 'In fact it's a privilege for us to be here on these beautiful islands, this perfect sea. I love it.'

She plunged back into the water and swam ahead of him, her pale limbs ethereal in the translucent water. He stayed a few strokes behind her so he could enjoy watching her swim.

He had never shared moments like this with either of his dreaded ex-wives. In fact he'd never shared moments so perfect and harmonious with anyone else—only that vibrant nineteen-year-old, so long ago in the waters of Santorini.

Now, as then, Claudia got the same enjoyment as he did from nature, good music, simple food well cooked and the company of friends. She even seemed to enjoy his tales of Ancient Greece. He reckoned she'd got more pleasure from the sight of a small pod of dolphins swimming alongside the *Daphne*, leaping out of the water, than ex-wife number two had got from yet another of the diamond bracelets she had demanded.

That wasn't to deny his privilege in swimming around a private island and never having to worry about money. Or the fact that, elegantly dressed, Claudia might very well like a diamond bracelet. In fact he would get one made for her to celebrate the birth of his child. Hell, why not get one to celebrate her pregnancy? But all his money hadn't bought him harmony such as he shared today with Claudia.

Back then, he had initiated Claudia into the joys of swimming in Greek waters, and he couldn't help thinking of what fun it would be to teach their child. Together. Perhaps more than one child...

He pinpointed just why he was enjoying her company so much—it was because they had so much in common, liked doing the same things. That had not been the case with his ex-wives. Could there be a chance that marriage would work for him after two such dreadful mistakes? A marriage that would secure the company of his child not just at weekends and school holidays but every day?

He took a few powerful strokes to take him ahead of Claudia, then slowed down so she would ease up too and the swim would take longer. He didn't want this perfect time to end. Not just the swim but her time on the island. She'd been, here with him on Kosmimo for a week now. He only had three more days left with her. It was going too fast. This magical time was ebbing away too rapidly. All too soon, real life would intervene. The life she would live in London and he in Athens, with too much distance between them.

He realised he was beginning to trust her.

Perhaps there could be another way forward. He didn't want to let her go.

The *Daphne* was anchored at one of the small islands that inhabited the seas near Kosmimo. It seemed to Claudia like a particularly lovely part of Ionian paradise. In fact it was utter bliss—not least because of the company. This morning she and Stefanos had swum right around the island. They'd been entertained by the wild goats clambering up clifftops.

They'd planned a whole day exploring away from Pevezzo Athina—just the two of them. Stefanos intended to sail to a taverna on another island, accessible only by sea, for lunch, then go elsewhere for the afternoon—perhaps for a spot of snorkelling.

Now, she lay on a deck chair in the shade on the mahogany deck of the *Daphne* and watched Stefanos as he polished some of the yacht's metalwork. She was sure he must have people he paid to maintain the boat—after all, he owned a fleet of luxury charter yachts, moored all around the Mediterranean—but he'd told her he liked to do the work himself. The *Daphne* had been a gift from grandparents who had both passed away, and he cherished it.

The boat was special to her too, for all the

memories it held of that summer she'd spent with him. And now she was making new memories.

She'd never been happier—or not since the time she'd spent on board the *Daphne* with Stefanos ten years ago. Each day had been an opportunity to explore Kosmimo and the surrounding islands, to relax in the luxury of the resort, to share meals with Alex and Dell, who had so quickly become good friends.

But in three more days, on Friday, the helicopter would come to take them back to Athens, where Stefanos would stay while she flew back to London. She dreaded the thought of the helicopter, although her morning sickness was more under control now. More than that, she dreaded the thought of not seeing Stefanos again until her twelve-week scan.

That was if he could make it. If he didn't change his mind about getting involved in the nitty-gritty of pregnancy. If business didn't get in the way. If he didn't meet a woman in the meantime—someone who wouldn't want him to have anything to do with a pregnant former lover in London.

Claudia batted the thoughts away as if they were a swarm of sandflies. She had to trust him. If she didn't she would drive herself crazy.

She got up from the chair to get a drink. As she did so, her white hat was caught by a sudden gust of wind and flew off her head and into the water.

'My hat!' She started to pull off the shirt she wore over her swimsuit. 'I'll go in and get it.'

'Wait! I'll grab it with the boat hook.' Stefanos reached over the side of the boat with the pole. 'Got it.' He dropped the sodden hat on the deck.

'Thank you. That's a useful hat. I won't be able to wear it until it dries, though.'

'There are other hats on board,' he said. 'Look in the closet in the galley.'

The interior of the *Daphne* was like a luxuriously appointed apartment. The kitchen might be called a galley, but it was full-sized. She found the closet and several hats inside, stacked on a shelf. They seemed to be men's hats, too big for her, but right at the back, almost as if it had been hidden, was a straw hat that looked smaller.

As she pulled it out, she gasped.

Her hat.

The battered straw hat she'd worn all that summer, bought at a market stall the first day she'd arrived, all fresh and eager for her job at the bar. Her initials were marked on the label, and a single long strand of auburn hair was caught in the weave. She'd left it behind somewhere in Santorini. When she'd got back home it hadn't been in her luggage, and she hadn't been able to remember where she'd last worn it. For a long time she'd mourned the loss of that hat.

Now she straightened the edges, put it on her head. It still fitted perfectly. Her favourite hat. She got some drinks from the refrigerator and headed back to the bow.

As she approached him, Stefanos stopped what he was doing to stare at her. 'You found your hat. I should have realised—'

'Realised what?'

'That you would find it where I'd hidden it.'

'Hidden it? Why would you do that? I assume I left it here on the boat ten years ago and you shoved it in the closet.'

He put down the polishing cloth he'd been using. 'You didn't leave it on the boat. The last time you wore it was that day when you got into my car and I took you to the airport. After you'd gone, I found it on the floor of the car. I picked it up and…and I held it close. The scent of your shampoo still lingered on the straw.'

She felt the smart of tears. 'Oh, Stefanos, that's so sad. To think at the same time I was crying my heart out and making an exhibition of myself in the airport. Remember I told you?'

'Yes,' he said.

'I cried until I didn't have a tear left. I wish I'd known you had my hat.'

'I took it home to Athens with me. Kept it in

my bedroom for a long time until I got engaged to Arina. It didn't seem fair to her for me to hang on to something that had belonged to my first love, the English girl who had let me down so badly, but I couldn't bring myself to throw it out. The next time I came to the boat I put it in that closet, right at the very back. It was your hat. I didn't want anyone else wearing it.'

'And it's been there for all these years?'

'I'd forgotten all about it until just now, when I suggested you look in there for a hat. I hoped you wouldn't find it…or that if you did you wouldn't recognise it.'

She frowned. 'Why?'

He shrugged broad shoulders. 'I didn't want you to think me stupidly sentimental.'

'I don't think it's stupid at all—what you did was beautiful. If I'd known, perhaps it would have given me some comfort to know I'd meant more to you than your thorough ghosting of me indicated.'

He reached out and touched the brim of the hat. 'Only now, seeing you wear this hat again, do I realise just how much you meant to me. How much I threw away by breaking off all contact with you. How stubborn I was—how arrogant to think there was only my way of doing things.'

'Stefanos, we were young, and it was so long ago, but knowing you kept this hat for ten years means a lot. It…it goes a long way to healing old wounds.'

She took the few steps across the deck to him. She put her hands on his shoulders and kissed him. He tasted of salt and lemon, memories and possibilities, his beard soft against her face. How many kisses had they shared on this boat? How many more would they share? She was leaving— going back to everyday life in London. This 'dating' time had made her realise she already knew everything she needed to know about Stefanos. And their time together was running out.

He took off her hat—that so-important hat. 'Please don't let it fly into the sea,' she said.

'Never,' he said, and he folded her hat and shoved it in the pocket of his shorts. It really wasn't meant to be folded, but it had been done so many times before, ten years ago.

He brushed his fingers through her hair and she sighed at the pleasure of it.

He wore only his shorts, his chest bare, strong and muscular and tanned. His skin was warm from the sun, smooth over hard muscle. He pulled her close…so close she could sense the hammering of his heart, feel his arousal. She bucked her hips against him in reply and kissed him again, hard and hungry and urgent.

He broke the kiss and pulled away. 'We have

to stop,' he said, his voice hoarse, his breath ragged.

'Why?'

'Because you said—'

'I've changed my mind,' she said.

'You're sure?'

'Absolutely sure.'

They strained against each other as their kiss grew in intensity. He slid her shirt up and off her, until she was left in just her swimsuit. He slid the straps down off her shoulders to free her breasts.

'Definitely bigger...' he breathed.

And more sensitive. Desire throbbed though her as he caressed her, his hands sliding down to cup her bottom. All she could think of was Stefanos and how much she wanted him...how much she had wanted him from the moment she'd first seen him...how much she would always want him. Was she fated only ever to want this one man with this all-consuming passion?

'Shall we take this inside?' he said. 'Although we didn't always.'

Many times they had made love out on the deck, their naked bodies silvered by moonlight.

'Inside might be more private than the deck if boats or helicopters come by,' she said, scarcely able to catch her breath. 'A cabin, maybe?'

'A cabin it is,' said Stefanos, and he swept her

up into his arms as if she were weightless and carried her inside.

They didn't make it past the saloon—the living area. Once he started touching her she was gone. He made pulling down her swimsuit into a caress, sliding his hands over her body exactly as she liked it. And as she stepped out of the swimsuit he took the opportunity to kiss her intimately, using his tongue and lips to bring her to a peak of arousal.

'I want *you*,' she said, as she tugged off his shorts, her hands clumsy with haste, and pulled him down onto the sofa with her.

She loved him. She had loved him from the moment she'd first met him. She had never stopped loving him. The reason she had never loved another was because no one was him. She couldn't bear the thought of life without him. How had it taken her so long to realise that?

'Is it safe?' he asked. 'For the baby, I mean.'

'Perfectly safe. The doctor assured me.'

Stefanos didn't give in to her demands to take her fast and furiously—rather he teased and tormented her with his clever fingers, before finally pushing gently into her, stroking slow and even, until they both caught the same rhythm of extreme pleasure. He knew just the right moment when she was on the edge to increase the pace. They climaxed together, and as Claudia looked up into his face, as she cried out his name, he was looking down, his eyes searching hers.

She let herself hope against hope that he might love her like she loved him.

She tried to stay awake. She wanted more lovemaking…wanted to talk to him about what had just happened between them…but she slid into sleep.

She woke to find Stefanos sitting on the edge of the sofa and gazing down into her face. He was wearing a towel around his hips. He was so handsome… She could never have enough of seeing his face so close. The flecks in his eyes seemed very green. She looked up at him and smiled a slow, lazy smile of completion and satisfaction. She reached her arms above her head and stretched like a cat.

He brushed her tousled hair away from her face. She caught his hand and kissed it.

'We always got that right, didn't we?' she said. 'The sex, I mean.'

'Always,' he said.

'Perhaps that's why we never talked much— we were too busy making love at any opportunity.' She stretched again. 'How long have I been asleep? I must have been tired out from the swim.'

And the wonderful, wonderful sex.

'Not long. You were smiling in your sleep. I think you were dreaming of good things.'

'I was dreaming of us swimming in a beautiful aquamarine sea like this one. We were naked and heading towards a happy place... I don't know where.'

'Sounds perfect to me,' he said.

'There was a baby mermaid swimming between us.'

'A mermaid? That must mean a little Dimitra is on her way to us.'

'Maybe not a mermaid. You can't really tell with a merbaby. This one had short baby hair floating around its head—black, by the way, so it could have been a merboy.'

'I guess we'll have to wait and see.' He smiled—indulgently, she thought.

'Am I making sense?' she asked.

'Kind of. I believe in fate; you believe in mermaids.'

'I... I want to believe that dreams can come true,' she said.

He dropped a kiss on the corner of her mouth, then looked back into her face. 'I think we should get married.'

Claudia stared at him. She sat bolt-upright, clutching the cotton throw from the sofa to cover her. 'That came from nowhere,' she said, not certain whether his tone of voice should lead her to feel excited or otherwise.

'I've thought about it a lot since we've been on the island. It seems the right thing to do.'

His tone was very serious. Not proposing-to-the-woman-he-loved serious, but business-proposal serious.

'The best thing for the baby. And for us. We get on so well with each other. We're great in bed.'

He might as well have summed up the pros of his proposal in point form. Which made her think about the cons.

Claudia swallowed a hit of intense disappointment. She hadn't expected or wanted a proposal—especially this kind of pragmatic proposal. But she had hoped for words of love.

While they'd been making love she'd desperately wanted to tell him how much she loved him, that for her first love was true love, but she'd known it wasn't the right time. Thank heaven she hadn't gasped out those words when he didn't appear to be thinking the same way. That would really have been making an exhibition of herself. She'd been fooled by the way he had looked into her eyes when they came together. Fooled into thinking that he might feel the same. Seemed she had misread him—big-time.

'What do you mean "the right thing to do"?'

'It makes sense. We're having this baby to-gether so we should be together. You being in London and me in Athens doesn't make sense.'

No, no, no. This wasn't how it was meant to be. He was supposed to say he loved her and couldn't live without her. *She couldn't settle for less.*

'Our current situation makes sense to me,' she said. 'We can legalise the arrangements we've discussed if you'd feel better doing that. You don't have to marry me to be a father to our child.'

She realised she was holding her shoulders up near her ears and forced herself to relax them.

'But surely it would be better for the child and easier for us to be married?' he said.

'I don't agree,' she said.

Couldn't he see he was offering marriage for all the wrong reasons? A proposal that was all about what would make life *easier* with the baby and nothing about *her.* He was offering her a loveless marriage. What made him think she'd even contemplate such a trap?

'Why not?' he said, dark brows drawn to-gether. 'You love it here. You'll love my house in Athens. You could even work with Alex and Dell on the resort if you wanted to—I'm sure they'd like to have your input.'

All that would be wonderful if it was in the context of a loving marriage, rather than a convenient arrangement between two people who were compatible in bed. Worse, he assumed she'd move to Greece without even asking her thoughts on such a move.

'I actually have my own business in London, thank you,' she said, trying desperately to keep her voice without a wobble.

'Didn't you say you'd had an offer to franchise it?'

'An offer that we may or may not consider.'

'You wouldn't need to work at all if we were married.'

Never had he sounded more arrogant. He must be very used to getting his own way. Was she seeing *that* Stefanos, born to privilege and wealth, here on Kosmimo? A Stefanos who would charm her into doing what was most convenient for him—that was put her life on hold to suit him and ever so conveniently have his child close by. The child she suspected he wanted to possess for himself.

'I have never wanted to not work,' she said. She spoke through gritted teeth, but he didn't seem to notice her tension. 'I think you know that.'

'You might feel differently after you've had the baby.'

He looked shocked that she hadn't immediately jumped on his proposal. He really thought he was doing the right thing. But he couldn't offer her love. And marriage without love, no matter how convenient, could not be considered.

'And I might not.'

'Dell and Alex really like you, and I know they'd want you to be part of the family.'

'My child will be part of your family by blood. I assume I might have some status in it as his or her mother, married or not.'

'It would be better for our child to have a mother and father married and living together.'

'Didn't you yourself point out how unhappy a person can be within a marriage? How good would it be for a child to have unhappily married parents?'

'Have you been unhappy with me this week?'

His question tore at her heart. She had never been happier. She was in love with a man who seemed dedicated to pleasing her and it had been heaven. But it seemed his dedication to her pleasure had been simply a means to an end.

'On the contrary, I've been very happy. But this is a holiday. It comes to an end on Friday.' She was finding it more and more difficult to speak calmly and give rational, reasoned answers.

'So why don't you want to marry me?' he said.

Claudia stared at him in total and utter disbelief. 'I don't get it,' she said. 'I really don't get it. Why this sudden turnaround from being a man who has repeatedly told me how ghastly his ex-wives are, how terribly they wounded him and how he never wants to get married again. Why are you messing with me like this, Stefanos?'

He looked genuinely bewildered, but she was too furious to care.

'I'm not messing with you,' he protested. 'If that's what—'

'What about *me*?' she said, glaring at him. 'What about what I want? My needs? Me being someone more than a sex partner and the mother of your child? Not once in all your talk of marriage have you asked how I see *my* future.'

She got up from the sofa, hastily tucked the throw around her, and stalked up and down the length of the saloon as she tried to gather her thoughts through a red mist of anger.

He stood up to face her. 'I'd hoped you'd see your future with me,' he said. 'Me and our child. Perhaps more children if we are blessed that way.'

She gritted her teeth. 'You really don't get it, do you? Is this an elaborate plot to get your hands on our baby just for yourself? Are you going to kick me out of the way in a third divorce and keep the baby?'

He went very still. Her words had obviously hurt him, and that pained her, but she had to get through to him.

'You know that's not true,' he said.

'*How* do I know? I don't know anything of what you're feeling apart from your wanting marriage as a practical transaction for the two of us. I'm puzzled why you would propose to me like that and expect me to be overjoyed. I don't think it's a language barrier. It's…it's more an emotional barrier you don't even know is there.'

'I don't know what the hell you're talking about,' he said, jaw clenched.

Claudia knew she couldn't keep this up any longer. She couldn't—*wouldn't*—let herself burst into tears of disappointment and misery.

'I'm sorry, Stefanos. I don't want to get married. I didn't ten years ago and I don't now. I appreciate that you want to do what you think is best for our baby, and I thank you. But let's keep the arrangement as it currently stands.'

He frowned. 'I don't understand… We're back where we were ten years ago.'

'Actually, the circumstances are very different,' she said, barely able to keep her voice even. 'I… I think you'll come to see that.'

In the meantime, she was trapped with him on his boat. If they'd been nearer to Kosmimo she'd have swum back to the resort. Where she'd be trapped with him in his villa. How had she got herself into this? How would she get back to London? She wouldn't be able to ask Alex or Dell. And she didn't want to embarrass herself or Stefanos.

She walked towards the smallest of the cabins. 'I'm not feeling well and I'm going to lie down. I'm sorry, you'll have to count me out for lunch and for snorkelling. Can you please take me back to the resort?'

She couldn't keep her voice steady enough for speech for a moment longer.

'Of course,' he said, tight-lipped.

As she walked past Stefanos, trying desperately not to show how upset she was that she had fallen back in love with him when he wasn't in love with her, she noticed she had thrown his shorts on the ground in her frenzy to get them off him. Her old straw hat had fallen out of his pocket and now lay on the floor.

She felt like kicking it.

CHAPTER SIXTEEN

STEFANOS DID NOT know where he'd gone wrong. Claudia hadn't come out of the cabin until the *Daphne* was back moored in its dock at Pevezzo Athina. Once back on land, she'd walked up to the villa next to him with only the minimum of polite exchanges, her voice completely lacking its usual warmth. Unless he'd said anything she'd lapsed into silence. Once inside the privacy of the villa she had reiterated that she wasn't feeling well, then disappeared into her suite with a supply of those darn crackers. Not once had she met his eyes.

He could hear her now, quietly sobbing in her suite, and it was tearing at his heart. She sounded so utterly miserable, and he had the gut-wrenching feeling it was all his fault. What had he done to offend her so badly? He had overcome all his dread of marriage and asked her to marry him. Why had that been so badly received?

He paced the length of the living room in the

villa. Back and forth, back and forth. Maybe she could hear his footsteps and it was scaring her. He cursed under his breath in Greek. Surely she didn't think he'd hurt her? *Never.* He wanted to protect her and never, ever hurt her. Although somehow he seemed to have grossly hurt her feelings.

He gave the pacing a break and headed to his suite to change into fresh white shorts and shirt. When he came back out her door was still closed, although thankfully her sobs had died away. He wasn't good with women's tears—didn't know how to handle them.

He was worried about her. What if she really wasn't well and it wasn't what he'd said that had upset her? Did he need to helicopter her to hospital? He couldn't bear it if anything were to happen to her; he felt overwhelmed by the reality of how important she was to him. It wasn't just about the baby. It was *her.* After these idyllic days together, he could not imagine life without her. Yet she was as uninterested in marrying him as she had been ten years ago, even though she was pregnant with their child.

He stood outside her closed door. Had he given up too easily? Today on the boat, seeing her in her battered old hat, it had been as if those ten years had rolled away and it was like it had been back then, when they were crazy for each other and no other person in the world had existed. It had been him and her, together in their bubble, and he wanted that again. Now he knew for sure it wasn't just about the sex—albeit mind-blowing. He felt more comfortable in her company than with any other woman—hell, with any other person. He wanted to make her his.

But had he lost her?

One thing was for sure: he wouldn't be ghosting her and spending another ten years in the wilderness without her.

He tried to ignore the inconvenient fact that she appeared to be ghosting him.

He looked at his watch. She'd been locked away in her suite for half an hour. He knocked on the door, expecting to have to bang hard. But the door swung open at his touch. She wasn't in the bedroom. The bathroom door was open, but she wasn't in there. Or in the walk-in closet.

Claudia was gone. There was just a lingering trace of her scent on the air, mixed with the tang of ginger. She must have sneaked out when he was in his own suite. She'd run away from him.

The realisation was like a kick in the gut.

But where had she gone? He gathered his senses enough to note that her clothes were in her closet, the swimsuit and white cover-up shirt she'd worn on the boat in the bathroom. She hadn't left the island—she actually *couldn't* leave the island, as it was only accessible by boat or helicopter. Dear heaven, he hoped she hadn't tried to take a boat out by herself. He froze at the thought. Then realised that whatever she might think of him, she wouldn't do anything that might put the baby in danger.

Dell. She had probably gone to Dell. They'd become close in the time he and Claudia had been here. She would certainly seek help from Dell. Although the reason *why* she needed help continued to evade him.

Would she have gone to the hotel? No. She knew Alex and Dell had lunch at home with their young children whenever they could. Claudia would have gone to their house.

When he got there, maybe he pressed too long and too hard on the bell, because Dell looked concerned when she opened the door. 'Stefanos. Are you okay? Is Claudia okay? The baby? Is everything all right with the baby?'

'Claudia isn't here? I thought she'd be here.' He ran his hands through his hair.

'Come in,' Dell said, practically dragging him inside. 'What's going on?'

'I don't actually know,' he said, hating to admit it.

'I saw Claudia out for a walk a little while ago. I asked her if she was okay. She said she was fine, but she didn't look fine to me. She said she just needed some fresh air, but she'd obviously been crying. I tried to coax her into telling me what was wrong but she wouldn't tell me. She's very loyal to you, you know.'

Alex joined them. 'What's the drama?'

'Stefanos is looking for Claudia, but Claudia doesn't seem to want to be found. He thought she'd be here.'

'Why would she be here?' Alex said. 'Weren't you and Claudia meant to be out on the *Daphne* all day?'

'We were—until she wasn't well and wanted to come back,' said Stefanos.

'Why?' said Dell. 'I thought her morning sickness was getting so much better.'

'It was. It is. It wasn't—'

'Wasn't morning sickness?' said Dell.

'No. She…uh…wasn't very happy with me.'

'What's going on, cousin?' asked Alex. 'You and Claudia seemed to be getting on so well.'

'We were hoping for an engagement before you left the island,' said Dell.

'So was I,' said Stefanos.

It had taken him a while to come round to the idea of marrying again, to let down those barriers. But now there was nothing more he wanted than to make Claudia his wife. For life.

'So what went wrong?' said Alex.

'And why is Claudia walking around the gardens crying?'

'I have to go and find her,' Stefanos said.

Dell put her hand on his arm. 'I don't think so. Not just yet. You need to think about how you're going to make things right with her.'

'What happened? Just tell us straight,' said Alex.

'I asked Claudia to marry me.'

'That's wonderful,' said Dell, beaming.

'I thought so,' he said. 'But it didn't go down well.'

'What do you mean, it didn't go down well?' said Dell.

'Basically, she said no.'

'She said no? I don't believe that,' said Dell. 'She's obviously in love with you. She's having your baby and she said no?'

Claudia was in love with him? Why hadn't she told him?

But she had...in so many ways, when he thought about it. Why hadn't he told her he loved her? That he had always loved her?

'*How* did you ask her to marry you, cousin?' said Alex.

'On bended knee?' asked Dell.

'No,' he said. 'I just said we should get married.'

He wasn't going to tell them he'd been on the

sofa with her, having just made love to her. That was his business. His and Claudia's.

'So, no flowery proposal?' said Dell.

'What did she say when you told her you love her?' said Alex.

'I didn't.'

There was silence from his cousin and his wife. 'You didn't tell her you love her?' said Dell in disbelief.

'Have you *ever* told her you love her?' said Alex.

Stefanos nodded. 'Back then. In Santorini.'

'Ten years ago?' said Alex. He put his arm on his cousin's shoulder. 'Do you realise how that sounds?'

'Yep. I'm beginning to.'

What a fool he'd been. So busy protecting himself from getting hurt he'd opened himself up to worse—losing Claudia.

'You got tricked into marriage the first time, and pretty much tricked into marriage the second time. Your track record for picking Mrs Right isn't great, is it?' Alex put up his hand. 'You don't have to answer that.'

'I will answer it. You're correct,' said Stefanos.

'We know you were hurt,' said Alex, obviously casting himself in the older cousin role.

But he had gone through real tragedy and

come through to give his heart to Dell. So Stefanos listened—his advice would be welcome.

'And you were wounded,' said Dell.

'You put up barriers,' said Alex. 'But you've got to get past that now.'

'Is Claudia the genuine Mrs Right for you?' said Dell.

'Yes. She was right for me ten years ago, when I stupidly lost her, and she's right for me now. No one could be more right.'

His words solidified into the absolute truth.

'I'm taking a guess she might think you asked her to marry you because of the baby, not necessarily for her,' said Dell. 'No woman in love wants to hear that. Do you want to lose her, Stefanos?'

'No!' His life would be empty without her in it.

'Then you have to reassure her that you love her and don't want to marry her just to give the baby your name.'

Surely she wouldn't have thought that?

He remembered her last angry words.

He'd got that wrong too.

'Don't let Claudia go,' said Alex. 'You've got to let her know how you really feel. You've made a mess of this, mate. You need to go to her and fix it. Be vulnerable and lay your heart on the line—difficult as that might seem.'

Stefanos didn't consider himself to be a humble type of person. But he knew he had to humble himself in front of Claudia.

'Do you think she'll have me?' he asked. 'After I screwed up the proposal?'

'That's entirely up to you,' said Alex. 'Only you can make this right. I suggest grovelling might be required.'

His cousin grinned. He was enjoying this. There was nothing like a Greek family for support.

'Okay…if required.' Not only would he humble himself, but grovel.

'Seriously, mate, I reckon you and Claudia could be very happy. She's a gorgeous girl in every way. The baby is a bonus.'

Dell's phone rang and she went over to the table to pick it up, turning her head away from the two men.

When she'd terminated the conversation she turned back to them. 'That was Claudia. She told me she's sorry for having worried me, but she's perfectly fine and is back in her suite.'

Stefanos had already turned to leave the room. 'Wish me luck,' he said. 'And thank you.'

This time he knew Claudia was in her suite. He was going in. Armed with a packet of organic crackers and a bottle of cold ginger drink, he knocked on the door.

'Claudia, are you okay?'

Silence.

'I heard you sniff,' he said.

'No, you didn't.'

'Okay, I heard you snore. I was being polite,' he said.

'You must be hearing things because I wasn't asleep.'

'You're awake now. How do you know you didn't drift off to sleep and start snoring?'

'Because I don't snore!' she said.

'Can you be one hundred percent sure of that?'

'Why are you standing there on the other side of the door insulting me?'

'I wouldn't be if you let me in. I have a cold ginger drink for you. And your favourite crackers. It's past lunchtime.'

The door opened and Claudia peered around the door. 'I doubt I will ever eat a cracker again after this.'

Her face was pale, the scattering of freckles across the bridge of her nose and across her cheeks standing out. He had kissed those freckles one by one just this morning. Her eyes were reddened, as if she'd been crying, and her hair was still tousled and full of salt. She looked vulnerable, sad, and he felt a fierce urge to protect her. But he knew he had caused her defences to go up and that she wouldn't welcome him pulling her into his arms.

'Are you going to let me in?' he said.

Without a word, she swung the door wide. He handed over the drink and the crackers and went through. He stepped further into the room. The bed linen was rumpled, as if she'd been lying down. Her laptop was open on the desk, with sheets of the resort notepaper beside it, covered with scribbled notes. She'd been busy since she'd come back from her walk.

'What are you doing?' he said, with a creeping sense of foreboding.

She seemed edgy, distracted, not wanting to meet his eye. 'I'm trying to find a way I can leave here before Friday. By myself.'

Stefanos stared at her, disbelief, pain and anguish roiling through him. 'Why would you do that?'

She picked up a piece of paper from the desk, screwed it up, put it down again. 'Because I don't think I can endure even another few days here. It's too uncomfortable for me, now I've said I won't marry you. And awkward around Alex and Dell, who had such hopes for us.'

'Have you found a way to leave?'

If she had, he would use everything in his considerable power to block it.

She looked down at the laptop. 'Unfortunately, no.' Her voice dropped with despair. 'I don't have the resources for a helicopter, the public ferry to Nidri doesn't stop here, all the charter boats are booked out, and I don't want to involve Dell and Alex. I don't want to embarrass them—or embarrass you in front of your family.'

'I looked for you at their house. Dell said she saw you out walking.'

'So they know I don't want to marry you? They adore you and now they'll think me mean. How embarrassing.'

'Not embarrassing. A friendship based on a first meeting with you retching behind a bush can survive that. They care about you too.'

'Family always comes first,' she said, with a watery smile.

'Not always,' he said. 'You know you can't leave the island?'

She sighed. 'So it seems. But I should be able to leave if I want to. I'm a guest here, not a prisoner.'

'Of course you're not a prisoner—how could you even think that?'

She turned away. Perhaps she could hear the distress in his voice. 'I'm sorry. Of course I know that. I didn't mean it. You've all been very good to me here.'

'I couldn't bear it if you left.'

She didn't meet his eye. 'You'll be seeing me again. In London, remember? At the hospital for my dating scan.'

'You and me as part-time parents...' He reached out, put his hands on her shoulders. 'Haven't the last few days meant anything to you? Didn't this morning mean anything to you?'

'You mean our wonderful romp or your business proposal?'

At the coolness of her tone he dropped his hands. 'I know. I'm sorry. Looking back, I guess that's exactly what it seemed like.'

'I believe you thought it was a proposal of marriage.'

'I *did* ask you to marry me.'

'You talked about how marriage was "the right thing to do" in terms of convenience for you and our child. The fact that we get on appeared to be a bonus.'

Her voice wasn't as steady as she'd obviously hoped it would be.

'You've got it wrong,' he said, aware of the fear searing his voice...the fear that he had lost her.

She took a step back, turned away, and then turned to face him again. 'You know, I've never chased the idea of marriage—but I've never completely dismissed it either,' she said. 'You might have thought you were asking me to marry you. But I never heard one word about love. And to me the only reason to get married is if you're head over heels in love with the other person, and they with you.'

'I wouldn't have asked you to marry me if I didn't love you.'

'You talked about being "attracted" to me. You talked about us having interests in common. You talked about looking after me and the baby. But you never talked about love.'

Last night she'd wheedled him into watching a romcom on television. She'd sat next to him on the sofa and jabbed him with her elbow every time he'd dozed off. He'd told her he liked action movies, or arthouse films, but she'd kept on swooning over the romance of the movie, the crazy ups and downs of the plot that kept the hero and heroine apart until the end.

Romance.

'I didn't give you romance,' he said.

'Actually, you did. The way you kept my hat was incredibly romantic. But you didn't give me love.'

How to explain to her that he'd been so closed off to love for so long he didn't know how to express it—was deep-down scared to express it. That was the emotional barrier she'd accused him of erecting. But when he really thought about it, when he was with the right person—

and she'd always been the right person—it really wasn't so difficult at all.

It was all there in his heart, just waiting to be said. To the only Mrs Right.

Now it was not a case of knowing he had to tell her he loved her if he had any hope of winning her, it was a case of wanting to.

'I love you, Claudia,' he said, looking into her eyes so she couldn't doubt his message. 'I fell in love with you the moment I met you that night at the bar in Santorini. Maybe because we were young…maybe because we were on vacation and you were English and I was Greek…it seemed somehow fleeting, and I didn't fight enough for it. I wanted to marry you, but I let you go. Where was the sense in that? I could have waited for you to be ready.'

'Stefanos—'

'Let me finish. This has been a long time coming. I've been thinking about it a lot—in fact it's all I've been thinking about since we've been here. That first day here, when you were so unwell on the helicopter, when you fell asleep and I tucked you into bed, I knew I'd brought you home and I never wanted you to leave.'

She took his hand, clasped it in hers. 'I dreamed that you called me *koukla mou*, the way you used to.'

'It was no dream,' he said. 'I don't want to

marry you because it's the right thing to do because you're pregnant. Or to give our child my name and an inheritance. Or because it would make parenting easier. I want to marry you because I want to live with you and wake up beside you every day of our lives. Swimming around the island with you this morning, I knew I wanted that.'

She smiled a tender, warm smile. 'You realise you might have had a very different answer from me this morning if that was the way you'd proposed?'

'It was a mistake,' he said ruefully. 'I was subconsciously trying to protect myself, I think. After spending this time with you I've realised the mistakes I've made—the disastrous marriages, the relationships that went nowhere—were made because I was looking for you in other people, seizing upon things that reminded me of you which ended up being fool's gold. I've only ever loved one woman, and she's standing in front of me now, looking at me like I'm crazy.'

'Not crazy at all. Because I've only ever loved one man. First love was true love for me, and no one else could match up to you. I love you, Stefanos, and I've been aching to tell you so.'

'Why didn't you?'

'I wasn't sure you felt the same way.'

'Do you know now? Or do I need to keep on telling you?'

'Yes, to both questions. I do know now, and I couldn't be happier about it. But we need to keep on saying *I love you*. And showing each other too.'

'Will you marry me?' he asked.

Claudia looked up at him, her blue eyes warm with love and happiness and relief. 'Yes, yes, and yes again.' She flung her arms around him. 'I want to marry you not for practical reasons, nor because we're having a baby, but because I love you and I want to spend my life with you. I don't want to blow this second chance we've been given.'

He could not resist. 'Given to us by...?'

'Fate—I know,' she said, with a smile that warmed his heart.

Claudia pulled Stefanos's head down to hers for a kiss. They kissed long and tenderly, and her heart soared to a new level of joy in their togetherness. Tender kisses led to passionate kisses, and then they made slow, exquisite love. And this time when they came to their climaxes she didn't have to guess how he felt, because he whispered words of undying love and she whispered them back.

'Do you ever wish we had stayed together ten

years ago? Do you wonder how our lives might have been?' she murmured.

'No. Because we are the people we are now, and this time I know it's going to work for us. I want you by my side when you're an old lady with silver hair.'

'With our children and grandchildren around us,' she said. 'I love the idea.'

She lay nestled into his shoulder, within the protective circle of his arms. She couldn't imagine a place anywhere in the world she'd rather be. She and Stefanos had gone through so much angst and heartache to find their way back to each other. But maybe she'd had to see the world and satisfy her need for independence before she could return to him.

She'd worried back then that she'd lose her sense of self if she committed her life to another. But now she could see that rather than losing herself by being with Stefanos she would gain more, because they were pledging themselves to a life together. Two together and committed were stronger than two apart. Perhaps things had worked out the way they'd been meant to.

'Dell and Alex will be very pleased to hear our news,' he said.

'I think you're right.' She knew Dell would be thrilled to welcome her into the family.

'You know I meant it when I said there would

be a role for you here at Pevezzo Athina if you should want it.'

'As it is definitely my favourite resort in the world, I would love that. Being here has made me remember why I enjoyed working in hotels and hospitality.'

'You'll like my house in Athens, too. It's white marble and very modern and overlooks the sea,' he said. 'Although I'm sure you'll want to put your stamp on it. And there's the apartment in Bloomsbury too—although we might want to buy a house outside of London too. It depends on how much time you want to devote to PWP.'

'There's been an interesting development there,' Claudia said.

'The franchise opportunity?'

'Something different and quite out of the blue. We helped a very nice woman move house after an ugly and well-publicised divorce from her wealthy businessman husband. She gave up her career to raise their now grown-up kids, so was left with loads of money and not a lot to do. She moves in the same social circles as Kitty does now, and she discovered that Kitty wanted to devote more of her time to a charitable trust started by Sebastian's grandmother. She told Kitty she liked the way we ran PWP and asked if she could buy into the business—or even buy the business outright if that suited us better. Kitty called me yesterday to run the idea by me, and we've agreed it might be time to move on. The business has been good to us, and tided us over some difficult times, but perhaps we don't need it any more since our lives have changed direction.'

'Remember what I said about new challenges helping you grow?' Stefanos said. 'Now might be a very good time to free yourself to follow different interests.'

'Including motherhood?' she said. 'And being your wife?'

'I couldn't agree more,' he said, drawing her close for another kiss.

'There's one more thing,' she said. 'Can we get married as soon as possible? I have this thing... I don't want to look pregnant in my wedding gown.'

'That can be arranged,' he said. 'Whatever you, *agape mou*, my beloved, want. One final question: would you like a diamond bracelet for a wedding present?'

She shook her head. 'Thank you, but that's not really my thing. Some diamond earrings for the wedding might be nice, though.'

'You can choose whatever you want,' he said.

As she kissed him she thought about the night she'd seen that handsome, black-haired boy across the crowds of people in that popular bar. As their gazes had connected the chatter and buzz of the bar had fallen away. In that moment the world had rearranged itself and her entire life had changed.

Somehow they had found their way back to each other now, so they could live life together as husband and wife. This day was the start of that journey.

CHAPTER SEVENTEEN

CLAUDIA REMEMBERED HER first sighting of the little white church that sat serenely on the cliff-top, set apart from Pevezzo Athina. It had been from the deck of the *Daphne*. Who would have thought, just weeks later, she would be getting married to Stefanos in that very same church on the most perfect of summer days? Or that she, who had always said she didn't want to get married, would have flung herself with such enthusiasm into the preparations for her wedding.

She'd become a veritable Bridezilla, as Kitty had teased her.

Her friends in London had marvelled at how quickly she'd decided to get married, but she'd pointed out that Stefanos had first asked her to marry him ten years earlier. It had just taken her an awful long time to say yes, as he liked to explain.

Being a Bridezilla had been so much easier when her billionaire fiancé, with his influence and his bank account, had been able to overcome every hurdle towards holding a wedding in a hurry. It had been no problem for one of Athens' top bridal designers to make not only Claudia's exquisite white gown, but also dresses for her thirteen-year-old twin sisters, Lucy and Lily, for Kitty and Dell, and for the mothers of the bride and groom—both formidable ladies who were still reserving judgement on each other.

Claudia suspected that the battle lines would dissolve once her baby mermaid was born. Tests had shown they were to have a single baby, a daughter, who would be named Dimitra Anne, after both her grandmothers.

The reception had, thankfully, been taken out of her hands. It was to be held in Alex and Dell's beautiful home, catered by the resort's chefs, with wine from their own vineyard. She couldn't have had her wedding celebration in a place she loved more.

Now, on her wedding day, Claudia stood outside the tiny church with her bridesmaids clustered around her like beautiful blue flowers. Her sisters with their long blonde hair so lovely in pale blue... Kitty and Dell in a deeper shade of delphinium-blue. Claudia wore diamonds at her throat and at her ears, to match her solitaire engagement ring, and her attendants wore sapphire pendants and earrings—all gifts from Stefanos. As was Greek custom, she had greeted their guests on the way in, and now they were all waiting inside for her.

The tiny church was packed with friends and family. Inside, Stefanos waited for her, along with his best man Alex, and the Adrastos family priest from Athens, who would perform the traditional ceremony.

Her mother was to give her away.

'Ready, darling?' she said now, taking her daughter's arm. 'All I ever wanted was for you to find the kind of love I was fortunate enough to find twice. And now you're marrying your first love. He's an exceptionally wonderful man and I couldn't be happier for you.' She paused. 'And I promise never to ask again why on earth you didn't snap him up when he was twenty.'

Claudia had come so far she was even able to laugh at that with her mother as she hugged her.

The twins preceded her down the aisle, casting rose petals as they went. Then Kitty and Dell made their graceful way down. At last came the bride's turn. As Claudia walked slowly down the aisle next to her mother, smiling faces from both sides turned towards her. But she only had eyes for one face. The face of the man waiting for her at the simple stone altar—her husband-to-be.

Stefanos was wearing a white linen suit which perfectly suited his dark good looks. He caught sight of her and smiled, his love showing in his eyes. The only man she had ever loved…would ever love. Her heart leapt with joy.

Stefanos had always thought Claudia looked beautiful in white—going right back to the simple cotton peasant dress she'd worn in Santorini ten years before. But today she was breathtaking in her long wedding gown, elegant in its simplicity, made of heavy white lace with cap sleeves, the only colour being her vibrant hair under a lace veil. She carried a simple bunch of white flowers tied with white ribbon.

He could not believe his luck that she was to be his after all these years. Fate had finally smiled on him. First love had grown into for ever love.

The wedding service emphasised the intertwining of two lives through the blessing of rings, the two crowns attached by a single ribbon placed on their heads, and the ceremonial sipping of blessed wine. He welcomed the traditions and the values binding their families together.

Finally they were husband and wife, and the priest even allowed the not-so-traditional custom of kissing the bride.

'I love you,' Stefanos murmured against her

mouth. 'I can't tell you enough how much I love you.'

'I love you too,' she said. 'We can never, ever say it too many times.'

'And even more importantly we must show how much we love each other,' he said. 'Until death do us part.'

Holding hands, joyously smiling, they walked back down the aisle, taking their first steps towards the start of their new life together.

* * * * *

If you enjoyed this story, check out these other great reads from Kandy Shepherd

Second Chance with His Cinderella
From Bridal Designer to Bride
Their Royal Baby Gift
One Night with Her Millionaire Boss

All available now!